Damned if I do

<u>AS PIPPA LANGHORN</u>
Love to Hate You
Heat of the Moment

<u>AS ELIZABETH STEVENS</u>
the Trouble with Hate is…
Being Not Good
Popped
the Art of Breaking Up

Accidentally Perfect Books
Accidentally Perfect
Perfectly Accidental

Royal Misadventures
Now Presenting
Lady in Training
Three of a Kind
Some Proposal
Royally Unprepared
Royals in Dating

AVAILABLE ON WATTPAD
Austen Reimagined
Pride
Prejudice

the Danu Cycle
Gryffynhall
Elfhaven

the Damned Trilogy: Book 1

Damned if I do

ELIZABETH STEVENS WRITING AS
SCARLETT KNOX

Kinky Siren, an imprint of Sleeping Dragon Books

Damned if I do
by Scarlett Knox

Print ISBN: 978-1925928211
Digital ISBN: 978-1925928204

Cover art by: Izzie Duffield

To long, hot Australian Summers,
Preparing me for Hell since 1991.

Contents

1

Drake

I couldn't tell you how many women I'd been with that week alone. But then, time seemed to stand still down here. And there was little else to do if Dad wasn't sending me to kill or maim or collect. Not that the women had any complaints.

"Son!" the dude who was not winning father of the year yelled as he threw open my bedroom doors dramatically.

I sat up, the girls giggling as they tumbled to my sides. "What now?" I asked him.

"Human children would be expected to show their parents more respect than you get away without," he said, his voice low and deep.

"Human children are far more expendable than me, apparently."

His eyes glowed red as he glared at me.

I couldn't have told you if we looked similar, if we looked like father and son. He was *definitely* my father though – not sure where else I got what he termed 'made me special'. I didn't even know what he really looked like. But most of the time, he looked like a suave middle-aged man with a fondness for dress-ups and musical theatre.

"Leave us," he told the girls.

They scrambled out of my bed, picked up their clothes and ran out. I raked a hand through my hair and didn't move. The sheet covered my lower half, but I wouldn't much have cared if it didn't.

"What do you want, Dad?" I asked with a sigh. "More babies for eternal torment? Or, is it virgins today? The corruption of a powerful soul? Oh no, wait. They tend to do that all by themselves these days."

"When you're done with your sarcasm…" my father warned before he pinched the bridge of his nose. "You do not know how I regret the years you spent with your mother."

"You do not know how I regret the years I spent without her."

"It was the best for you."

"Your father, sir," Truman puffed as he skidded into the room.

"Yeah, I worked that one out. Thanks, lads," I said to him as Kyle and Ignacio ran into the back of him. I ignored the three devilbums and turned to my father again. "If I'm immortal, it was irrelevant, wasn't it?" I snapped. "I could have stayed with her through her natural life then come to you."

Dad held his hand up as though it was obvious. "It is unseemly for a Prince of Hell to be raised by humans!"

"Firstly, not technically a Prince of Hell. Secondly, maybe you should stop fucking random human women, then."

His glare hardened. "On the topic of unseemly, it is time you found a wife."

Well, that certainly hadn't been what I was expecting and it certainly shut me up. Kyle had his claws over his mouth in excited anticipation. Ignacio was watching the room with his usual state of distrust. Truman was standing patiently with his arms behind his back, rocking back slightly on his hooves. And my father and I just stared at each other for ages.

"Sorry. You, what?" I finally asked when he didn't elaborate.

"A Prince of Hell–"

"Not that kind of Prince…" I interjected with a mutter.

"A prince of Hell…" he paused for my approval and I nodded, "should be married. It's unseemly that my last living son is unmarried after all these years."

I'd been wondering when Dad was going to get his next big idea stuck in his head. It had been ages since he'd turned Hell upside down in the quest to see through his latest endeavour. It now seemed that his new endeavour was going to involve me and nuptials. Well, if I was going to be looking at Grandad knew how long of him annoying the Heaven out of me, the least I could do was annoy him a little first.

"Oh, Esther's kids will love that. 'Sorry, boys, no Christmas presents this year, I've just remembered you don't count'–"

"Would you shut up?" Dad sighed. But he tended to get that way at any mention of my step-mother. Although, was she really a step-mother if they were married *before* I was conceived…?

"Almost done. 'Why, Zael? Well, because Daddy only counts the bastard Nephilim children who all end up dying because Grandad's favourite sons despise their very existence. Oh no, wait. There's one more left and, to show just how much he means to me, I torment him along with all my other precious souls.' Did I miss anything?"

"Oh, only the part where you remember to show some holy respect to the man who gave you life. Other than that, faultless." Dad kissed his fingers at me in mock commendation.

"Your little criticisms are what help me grow as a person, Dad," I told him as I got up and looked for my trousers.

"If you're done?"

I waved my hand at him. "Yeah. All good. Continue."

"Right. So pleased. As I was saying, you're going to marry. I'll give you say…a week to think of someone. Otherwise, I've got some great candidates lined up. I was thinking a 'torture to the death', last one standing wins your hand!" He spread his hands out theatrically and I knew he was already picturing the staging and the costumes.

I pulled on my trousers. "Yeah, I'm going to take a hard pass on that. But thanks. You should still stage the show, though. It'd get a great turn-out."

The room's temperature rose significantly and I turned to see my father at his flamiest. Tall. Imposing. Bright red. Horns. Hooves. Wings. Fire just about everywhere like he'd gone overboard with the bedazzler again.

"Did I say something, Dad? You look a touch…irritated." Over the millennia I'd been stuck down there, I'd perfected the sarcastically simpering tone of concern.

"Uh, your devilness?" one of the guard demons poked his head into my room.

Dad lost a little of his pizazz and turned to see what the interruption was going to entail. "Yes. What?"

"Join the party, Neville," I offered, turning to look for a shirt but Truman was holding one out to me already. "Thanks," I said to him as I took it and shucked it on, keeping an eye on Dad and his guard as they whispered to each other.

Dad was looking agitated for a whole other reason now.

"What's up?" I asked.

"Escapee. You want to do something helpful today? Consider this your One Bad Deed." And with that, my father swept out of the room, expecting me to follow.

I took the proffered apple from Kyle and looked at the three devilbums who had, over the ages, somehow become my sort of servants I supposed.

"What do you think, boys? Shall we go see what the puppy caught for us?"

"See the puppy!" Kyle sang as he skipped out, Ignacio following behind with his usual string of muttered curses.

"Your father seemed particularly displeased today, sir," Truman said as we followed the other two.

"I'm getting married, Truman," I told him.

"I heard, sir. Mazel tov. Any ideas for the lucky soul?"

"No."

"Well, won't that be fun, sir?" Truman commented dryly and I would have laughed if I'd remembered how.

By the time we got to Cerberus' domain, Dad hadn't had any luck getting the great ball of fluff to do what he wanted. Kyle was dancing around, wanting to get closer to Cerberus, but also knowing the dog would try to eat him again if given the chance. And Ignacio was grumbling at Kyle to keep back so he didn't get eaten. Again.

I leant against the cavern wall, crossed my arms and watched the scene unfold, and Truman kept by my side as usual.

"Cerb, put the nice soul down," Dad commanded, pointing at the ground and Cerberus just growled around the soul in the mouth of the middle head, which we'd named Huxley. "Cerb, don't make me tell you again."

Cerberus just growled again and the soul sensibly just hung limply and waited for judgement. Souls had a tendency to look pretty similar down here, but I thought it was a bloke called Rene.

"Cerberus! You will do as you're told," my father tried on the big dog.

Unsurprisingly, that didn't work. So, he tried another tack.

"Who's a clever doggo, catching themselves a sneaky soul?" Dad asked, his voice rising at least one octave, if not two, as he slapped his knees excitedly.

Cerberus' tail wagged, but he didn't seem inclined to drop the soul.

"I see your domination of Hell is in top form today, Dad," I said as I bit into the apple.

He turned and glared at me, his eyes glowing red again. "Why thank you, Drake. As usual, your input is invaluable. Why don't you have a go? The mutt doesn't listen to anyone anyway."

The head we called Rocky snapped at Dad, who just managed to jump out of the way in time with a high-pitched yelp.

I pushed myself off the wall, knowing there was no way Cerberus was going to listen to me, but figuring I lost nothing by giving it a go. "Cerberus, your job is done. Drop the soul and I'll take him back to his torment."

Cerberus' tail thumped against the floor, sending wafts of dust and air at us. Rocky and the third head, Todd, looked to Dad almost smugly as Huxley gently dropped the soul on the ground in front of his massive paws.

"Oh, yes. Of course. You'll listen to *him*," Dad grumbled, throwing his arms up.

"Only to show you you're not the boss of him," I said.

"But I *am* the boss of him!" Dad whined.

And while I dealt with the soul – pulling him to his proverbial feet – Cerberus launched himself at Dad and sent him down in a pile of laughter. I dragged the soul out of the cavern while Cerberus licked Dad's face and Dad gushed over what a good boy he was.

"Thanks, Drake," the soul said forlornly. "Eternal torment's probably better than being shredded by the big guy, eh?"

"Have we learned our lesson, then?"

"Yes, sir. No more escaping."

"I remember you saying that a couple hundred years ago, Rene."

Rene shrugged. "Well, you know how it is."

I nodded. I did know how it was. Hell was a never-ending string of the same thing day in and day out, timeless while at the same time not. I guessed that was the point of eternal torment, though; it was boring in its monotony. But it just really didn't seem like any way to spend your best years of death.

"Where are you meant to be?" I asked him.

"Uh, it's Thursday afternoon? So, the Room of Perpetual Anguish."

By its name, you'd be forgiven for thinking we only had the one. We didn't. But you just knew stuff as the son of the Lord of Hell. Like, I knew exactly which Room of Perpetual Anguish Rene was supposed to be in on a Thursday afternoon – although, days were a loose construct down here. Just like, out of the nigh infinite number of souls and demons and creatures that wandered around Hell, I knew this one was Rene.

"You doing anything interesting this afternoon?" he asked as I dragged him along.

"No, not really."

"Same old, same old?"

"Story of my eternal life," I huffed and stopped as we got to the room. "Right. Have an infernal afternoon."

"Will do. You, too," Rene said with a nod and I threw him through the door while he gave the obligatory scream of suffering.

Then, I turned and looked around the hallway. "Right. What was I doing?"

"Finding a wife, sir," Truman said, from down by my leg.

I nodded and started walking to nowhere in particular. "Yeah, sure. Okay. Any ideas?"

"You had a good time with Hyrelle, if I remember rightly."

I did. "She's not exactly marriage material."

"No. Succubi usually aren't, sir."

"What's Ammit up to these days?"

Truman trotted by my side. "She still hangs out with Anubis, eating hearts, devouring dead. The same old schtick."

"Okay, so no way I'm getting between them, then."

"How about Lillith, sir?"

I shuddered. "And risk Samael kicking my arse again? Pass. Besides, I'd like to think we can find someone Dad hasn't fucked."

"That might be difficult, sir."

I sighed. "It might."

We did our usual inspection of Hell, doing the rounds and making sure the right souls were in the right places, as we tried to come up with a list of potential wives. Kyle got into his usual level of mischief, making sure Ignacio held him back while he (very convincingly) threatened a guard demon that he'd do a better job with a soul's torment. Except for the traditional moment Ignacio 'accidentally' let go and Kyle went running behind me for cover.

Finally, as I was assuring the guard demon that Kyle was just messing about as usual and wasn't worth the hassle of beating him to a mushy pulp (again), it came to me. It might have had something to do with the fact that the soul was moaning something about human weddings and I'd had a lightbulb moment.

"Truman! I've got it," I said as I nudged Ignacio away from the guard demon with my foot to stop him avenging the threat to Kyle's pulp.

I didn't need to hear Truman's sigh to know he'd rolled his eyes. "Got what, sir?"

"We don't need to find me a wife."

"We don't, sir?"

I shook my head. "No."

"I'm afraid I don't follow, sir."

"I'm technically already married!"

Truman's step faltered, then he hurried to catch up. "Already...? Did I miss something, sir?"

"No. That's the beauty of it."

"Sir… You don't mean…?"

I nodded. "Yes, Truman. I do." I chuckled. "Or rather, I did."

"But sir–"

"Are we going back up?" Kyle asked excitedly, bouncing on his little hooves.

"Yes, we are," I answered.

"Do you think that's wise, sir?" Truman asked.

"Wiser than me having a marriage down here."

Truman inclined his head. "Indeed, sir."

Kyle went running ahead, squealing happily, "Going back up the top! Have to tell the puppy!"

Ignacio gave a muttered huff and went jogging after him, ever the protector of Kyle's accident-prone pulp.

I looked down at Truman. "What are the chances of her being into orgies, do you think?"

"Slim, sir."

I ran my hand over my chin. "You might be right."

2

Wren

As I heard the toot of the horn, I checked my tie in the mirror one last time. As I tugged on it, my eyes slid to the picture tucked into the frame and I smiled as I ran my fingers over it fondly.

The horn blasted again, more urgently this time, and I laughed as I grabbed my bag and ran out of my room.

"She's been sitting out there for *hours*," my older sister whined from her perch at the breakfast bar, hands wrapped around her coffee cup like caffeine worked by osmosis. I knew she'd had a late one the night before, complete with too many shots.

Ah, the life of a uni student.

I chuckled as I grabbed my travel mug and kissed her cheek. "I suspect she'll think the same thing." I pointed at the coffee in her hands. "Only works if you drink it."

Tilly grunted like it was supposed to be words and shooed me out of the room.

Pulling the front door closed behind me, I waved to my best friend who was glaring at me from the driver's seat of her car. I shrugged unapologetically as I wandered down the front path and I saw her putting the window down.

"So help me, Wren! If you're not in this car in two seconds, I'm leaving without you," she snapped.

I smirked. "Oh, come on, Harm. We're not even late."

"Says you. Now, let's go!" She reached over and threw open the passenger door.

I dropped into it and that's when we saw the moving truck pull into our street.

"No one's sold lately, have they?" Harmony asked as I put my seatbelt on. She wrapped her hands around the steering wheel as she leant forward and squinted despite the glasses perched on her nose.

I looked back up to the truck and tried to work out which house it was going to stop at. "Not that I know of."

We sat watching and I tried not to laugh.

"I thought we were going to be late?" I hedged and Harmony frowned.

"Shut up," she muttered as she got the car started and we drove off without waiting to see where the truck stopped.

Harmony drove us to school, like she did every morning, and she couldn't stop talking about the moving truck. I got every possible scenario her mind came up with for what was in the truck, where it was stopping, why whoever had moved, and more. Most scenarios involved someone dying tragically and/or horribly – Harmony's favourite.

School wasn't my favourite place in the world. But then again, how many soon to be eighteen-year-olds thought it was? I wasn't particularly bad at school. I didn't mind learning. I had people I considered friends. I just felt…disjointed.

Everyone else had known exactly what degree they'd wanted to apply for. Everyone else knew what they were doing with their lives. Everyone else fit. I wasn't unhappy,

I just felt like something was out of place and I couldn't quite put my finger on it.

That day, Harmony mostly took my mind off it by still going on about the moving truck while I avoided running into people and failed to pay proper attention to where I was going or what I was doing. She shared her theories with our friends, who offered their own theories as well. There was the inevitable good-natured joke about my old neighbour moving back in and all the jokes that followed on after that.

I really shouldn't have been surprised that such a thing would hold their excitement and over-active imaginations all day. And Harmony was apparently still going on about it on the way home.

"The moving truck!" Harmony yelped.

"You still obsessed with that truck?"

"Um, yeah. Especially when it's pulling out of your neighbour's place," I heard Harmony say and looked up.

"The Petersons didn't move. Did they?" I asked.

"How would I know?"

I shrugged as I looked back at my phone. "Maybe they got a new couch?"

"That took all day to take inside?" She lost her scepticism as she added, "Moving people are very well known for their laziness."

I looked at her askance, my eyebrows narrowed. "Eight hours lazy, though?"

Harmony slowed to a stop as the truck finished pulling out of the Petersons' driveway in front of us. The truck then drove away, but Harmony did not get moving again.

"Have you forgotten which one's the accelerator?" I asked her.

"My grasp of the mechanics of operating this vehicle far outweighs your own. Much like my grasp of the important things in life. Case in point, the very fine specimen of man standing in your next-door driveway."

My eyes snapped up. Never let it be said that I missed an opportunity for a perve.

And it was anything but a missed opportunity.

The guy was crazy hot. Movie star hot. The kind of hot you didn't need to wait for him to smile, or look at the camera in total outrageous disbelief, or to get his top off. Guy was the sort of hot you knew he was going to turn out to be a bad guy at the end when your protagonist walks off happily into the sunset with the guy you only noticed was hot halfway through the story.

He was tall and obviously built under a tight white t-shirt and jeans. His super dark hair was short at the sides and swept to the side at the front. And he was looking right at us.

"Holy hot potatoes, cannelloni beans!" Harmony breathed.

It would be a total stretch to say there was anything normal about Harmony, and I wouldn't have her any other way. Besides, I was hardly in a position to judge normal.

I nodded. "You're not wrong."

"I call dibs."

"You can have him. But I gotta question how interested he'll be if we keep sitting in the middle of my street staring at him like we've never touched, let alone seen, a member of the male species."

"Wren, guys like that were not only designed to be ogled, they demand to be ogled."

I conceded. "All experience points to yes."

"So, let me ogle."

"Can you ogle once parked at the very least?" I laughed.

She huffed. "I suppose."

Harmony pulled up to the curb across from my house and we turned to see the guy next door was still staring at us. Only now, his expression was of amused interest. Which, you know, made him ten times hotter in a fantasy-only kind of way. Ain't nobody got time for that kind of ego.

"See," Harmony pointed at him. "He is eating up the being ogled."

"I do see. Super attractive."

"I know. He is."

"Sarcasm, Harm. Heard of it?"

"Guys like that don't need a personality," Harmony argued.

I snorted as I grabbed my bag. "No. You're right. Who wants a personality getting in the way?"

"Wren, a boy like that? He can be a wet towel for all I care."

"You're nasty," I chuckled as I opened the door and got out.

Harmony leant over to look up at me and batted her eyes at me adorably. "Oh, bless. I so love how you pretend you're not."

I stuck my tongue out at her. "I'll see you in the morning."

"Yeah," she scoffed sarcastically. "If you were on time."

I looked up coyly. "Buy me a clock for my birthday."

Harmony barked a laugh. "I'll get one of those ones with programmable tones."

"And have you yelling at me every morning?" I kissed my fingers. "Perfection."

"Bye!" she yelled as I closed the door.

I gave her one more wave, jogged across the street, then headed to the front door. As I went, I couldn't help but look over at the guy next door. Was it just me, or was it kind of weird that he was just standing there watching us? Was it creepy weird or like beginning of a grand romance weird? It certainly made me interested to know if he was a serial killer or just intensely sexy.

Him moving made me look at him properly and I saw he was walking to the fence. Like right towards me.

"Hey, neighbour," he said and his voice was deep and tantalising.

Many, many witty-verging-on-sexy comebacks shot through my head, but every single one of them tripped flat on their faces before they got to my mouth. So, all I could do was give him a terse smile and a nod as I pulled my bag further up my shoulder and hurried inside with my head down.

I heard Harmony toot the horn and I knew she was laughing at me. So, I shot her a grumpy glance as I shut the door.

3

Drake

I'd done the whole human thing – moving truck, friends to help me shift my crap inside, plenty of yelling and almost dropping things, and lots of the obligatory breakages. Granted, the whole thing was an elaborate illusion while the boys and I sat inside catching up on everything I needed to know to pass as a human. But it was the thought that counted.

After our Contemporary Life consultant left, I dropped back into one of the arm chairs and ran my hand over my jaw with a heavy sigh.

"Indeed, sir," Truman said. "The world is much changed."

I shrugged as I leant forward on my knees. "If I'm honest, I expected worse. But I guess twelve years isn't that much in the grand scheme."

"Certainly less than a fiery eternity," Truman commented and I nodded.

"You're not wrong."

"Might I ask, sir, how you plan to get her back home?"

"Ask all you like. I have no idea yet."

I heard Kyle squeaking in excitement and looked over to see him hanging onto the windowsill and staring out the front.

"What's that?" he asked, cocking his head to the side, his big ears flapping.

I flicked a hand at Truman as I sat back again. Truman hurried over to Kyle and I looked around to see where Ignacio had wandered off to. But I couldn't see the little grouch.

"What is it?" Kyle asked Truman.

Truman looked at me before he answered. "That is a cat, Kyle."

"Cat." Kyle tried the word on for size.

"Have you thought about how you'll broach the subject with her, sir?" Truman asked me.

"Not in the slightest. But when have I ever struck out?"

"No. Of course, sir."

"Can Kyle eat it?" Kyle asked.

I smirked at Kyle's utter naivety and obsession with animals. "No, you can't eat it. If you do have an idea for getting her home again, though, I'm open to all suggestions."

"What do with it then?" Kyle asked, still staring out at the window.

"Pets. Gifts," I answered sub-consciously as I saw Ignacio wandering in. "And where have you been?"

Ignacio pointed to the front door. "She's coming."

I rubbed my hands together excitedly as I stood up. "All right, boys. Game on."

"A hand, sir?"

"No." I shook my head. "You boys stay inside for now."

Calling the illusion together, I walked out the front door with the 'movers' and saw them off just at the right time that the truck would get in the girls' way. I set it up perfectly. A millennium with my father and at least I could say I was adept at showmanship if nothing else.

I watched the little hatchback slow to a stop in front of the truck in perfect place for the girls to be right in front of me. And both of them were looking right at me. The girl in the passenger seat, she was the one I was here for. But I couldn't quite see her past the girl in the driver seat.

But I saw enough to know they were both interested. Maybe my chances of an orgy weren't quite so slim after all.

I watched as her friend pulled up to the curb and they both looked back at me.

And I enjoyed it. Why wouldn't I? Two girls appreciating my fine form? I never got sick of it. Although, I wasn't convinced this particular time was going to end in significantly less clothes than were currently involved.

As she got out of the car, I half wished this whole thing wasn't going to be so easy. I almost planned on making the time to romance her the old-fashioned way. But it was unnecessary. She fulfilled my father's ludicrous request for a wife. One meet and greet with Pops and I was back to my old, never-ending, monotonous life. And she could go back to her easy, simple human existence.

Still, it was almost a shame.

She was in a hideous school uniform with her brown hair in a simple ponytail, but I could see she had the makings of gorgeous under all that. It was in the way she smiled at her friend, the way her eyes shone as she laughed, and the mischief in her crooked smile. My neighbour had definitely grown up in twelve years. And, if I wasn't already damned, I would have been if I said those twelve years didn't look good on her.

As she walked across the street, I pictured it all again.

The day had been lit with sunbeams, flowers spread across the field and danced in the sweet breeze, the stream had burbled happily beside me, and there she'd been with that smile. Her in that little white dress with a ribbon around her middle, a wreath of flowers in her mess of dark blonde curls, and a single wilting daisy in her hand as she ran through the flowers over to me. At eight, I'd thought it had been the stupidest thing in the world. But as stupid as I'd thought it, I could never say no to that smile.

All I needed now was for her to remember it.

"Hey, neighbour."

It was something I'd said to her hundreds of times. And every time, I'd been met with a wide smile, warm eyes, an open laugh, and an innocent excitement for a new adventure. This time, I got the cold shoulder. No. It was worse than the cold shoulder. All humour at her friend was gone and in its place was indifferent politeness as she hurried inside.

What the Heaven had happened to the bubbly little girl I'd left behind?

I looked to the friend in the car who grinned at me knowingly. Except I wasn't quite sure what she knew. I could make a few educated guesses – she was laughing over the fact I'd swung and missed, she was laughing over the fact my wife had rushed inside, she was laughing over the fact that… Yeah, I was out of ideas. For whatever reason she was laughing, she tooted the horn before she drove away.

"Well, that could have been worse, sir," Truman commented and I looked down at him.

"How?"

Truman rocked back on his hooves. "Well, she could have rejected you."

"What do you call that?" I asked him.

Truman frowned. "Sir, I know you're unaccustomed to not…scoring. But allow me to assure you that that display was not rejection."

"Really? And what was it?"

"That, sir, was nothing more than nervousness."

"Truman?" I asked as he started trotting back inside.

"Yes, sir?"

"Have you dated?"

"When would I have the time for dating, sir?" It was said in the sort of way we both knew he wasn't saying no, but he wasn't about to admit anything either.

I hurried after him. "Oh, I don't know. There was a time before me."

"Was there, sir?" I doubted I was imagining the wistful insolence buried in his voice.

"Where is she?" Kyle asked, bouncing up and down, and trying to look around me.

I dropped to one knee in front of him. "She's not coming today."

Kyle stopped and looked at me. His ears drooped and his bottom lip stuck out. "Why not?"

"His highness…struck out," Truman explained.

Kyle's eyes went wide and his claws went over his mouth.

I shook my head at him as I got up. "She was shy, that's all."

"What's your next move, boss?" Ignacio growled.

I shrugged. "I dunno."

"Might I suggest you try again, sir?"

I nodded to Truman. "Good plan."

"Indeed, sir," I heard Truman sigh. "In the meantime, I'll find something for dinner, shall I?"

"Cat?" Kyle asked happily and he skipped after Truman.

"Try again," I mused to myself as I took the stairs two at a time and walked into my old room.

From memory, it looked directly at the window to her bedroom.

I saw blue curtains fluttering in the breeze, but no sign of her as I tried to work out how best to try again.

And I spent the bloody whole week on it.

While she was at school, I did some research on what girls liked these days. The amount of drivel I ingested in the guise of books, movies and TV shows was enough to make a man sick. But I persevered, and found a few new things to add to my list of torture material.

On Tuesday, I was outside in the driveway working on my motorcycle in tight jeans and a tank top. I was smeared with grease and glistened with beading sweat in the unseasonable late-September heat. It was a classic move – by all accounts – and should have worked wonders. It should have been a homerun. But then her sister came home before her and I found myself politely trying to avoid her flirtation when the car pulled up outside their house.

Wednesday, I pulled out the big guns. By the time the girls were driving past, I was in the process of saving a kitten – Kyle in disguise – from the front tree. I was shirtless, of course. My unseemly muscles rippled with the slightest movement of my taut body. I climbed back down the ladder, cradling a very dedicated Kyle against my chest, and turned to see her standing in her front driveway practically drooling. But when I smiled, I still only received a terse smile in response before she disappeared inside.

I wasn't leaving anything to chance on Thursday. I kept an eye on their house the whole day. When her friend's car stopped at the curb, no one else was home. It was just her. The sister hadn't come home from uni yet. The parents were still at work. So, once she was inside, I got myself sorted, somehow convinced Kyle to stay inside, and went next door.

I smoothed my hair and pressed the doorbell.

"Just a second!" I heard her call, and the sounds of footsteps on the stairs.

She was smiling when she pulled the door open, but it fell when she saw it was me.

"Hi," she said slowly, looking around behind me.

"Hey, neighbour."

Still nothing. No recognition. All I got was a questioning expectation.

"Uh…" I started, then held up the plate of Apple Slice. "I just thought I'd be neighbourly and say hello."

She looked at the plate and then back at me. "Thanks."

I held the plate out to her and she took it. "I'm–"

Her phone rang and she looked at me sort of apologetically. "Sorry." As she pulled her phone out of her pocket with one hand and started closing the door with her foot, she held up the plate and said, "Thanks for these."

Then the door was closed in my face and I'd failed spectacularly.

I didn't know what was happening. Collection was in my genes. We go to Earth, we get the mortal, we bring them home. It's not like it was rocket science – we'd been doing it for hundreds of thousands of Earth's years. But somehow, I couldn't manage to get this one human to do my bidding.

On Friday, I was scraping the barrel.

As she walked up her path, I was collecting the mail and actually asked her, "How was school?"

Needless to say, that didn't work. She nodded politely while looking completely baffled as to why I'd be talking to her, and hurried inside.

As I walked back into the Petersons', I slammed the door and roared.

"How did it go, sir?" Truman asked blithely as I walked in.

"She coming home?" Kyle asked happily.

I shook my head. "I'm done. I'm out of moves. I'm out of patience."

"What's the play, boss?" Ignacio grunted.

"We're taking her tonight."

"You're just taking her?" Truman's tone had just enough distaste in it for me to know what even he, a hellspawn, thought of that.

"No. She has to come willingly, but I'm just going to give her the truth."

"Is that wise, sir?"

"I am all out of fucks on that one, Truman."

"What can we do?"

I looked out the front window and saw her father's car pulling into the driveway. "I need you to go to her and get her to come and talk to me."

"You think that will work?"

I shrugged and pointed at him. "She'll have to believe it when she's staring at the hot, red proof."

"Kyle go! Oh, pick Kyle!" he squeaked, bouncing up and down, his arm stretched above his head.

I gave him a rough approximation of a ghost-smile. "Thanks, man. But I think Truman's the devilbum for this."

Kyle sagged, but nodded.

"And what message would you like me to deliver, sir?"

"Just tell her we need to have a frank discussion."

Truman nodded. "Excellent, sir. I look forward to it."

"You think she'll just come?" Ignacio huffed.

I gave him my best stern glare. "I am my father's son. I always collect."

4
Wren

Why was it so hard to talk to attractive people?

It's not like I was shy.

It's not like I lacked self-confidence.

It's not like I couldn't think up a dozen dirty things I wanted to do before I knew a guy's name.

It was just, faced with all that hotness, all I got was a loss of brain to mouth connection. Which, in turn, led to the resting jerk face. Harmony and I called it jerk face because apparently I wasn't sexy-mean enough for it to be bitch face.

So, on Friday for the umpteenth time that week, I ignored the hotty next door as he quite clearly tried to talk to me and stomped up to my room. I flung my bag on the floor and something caught my eye enough to temper my mood somewhat.

It was the picture on my mirror.

I went over to it and pulled it down, flopping onto my bed to look at it.

I barely remembered the day it had been taken – all I had were memories based on what Mum, Dad and Tilly said about it – but I'd been thinking about it more and more in the last few days. Even though I couldn't trust my memories about how it all happened, I knew I could trust the memory of the way I'd felt. I'd felt amazing. I'd felt grown up. I'd felt understood. I'd felt like I wasn't just some stupid kid.

Looking back, it was stupid. Asking the boy next door to marry me? Especially when I'd been practically half his age – five to his eight, the scandal! But he'd said yes, the way he'd always said yes. These days, I knew it was just to humour me. But my friends and I always laughed at the pure romance in the idea that one day he'd come back and we'd–

I was distracted by a clattering noise behind me and I sat up quickly. My mind took a few seconds to work out what my eyes were seeing.

Trying to disentangle itself from the cord of my now broken lamp was a weird little thing. It was probably half my height, maybe shorter. Its lower half looked like goat legs – much like Mr Tumnus – covered with brown hair and ending in hooves. His top half was red leathery skin. Its hands only had three fingers and a thumb with sharp claws. It had a big head, with a wide mouth and a little brown goatee. Its ears were huge bat-like things and it had little black horns. And to top it all off, when it shifted as it finally got its hoof free of the cord, it had a thin red tail that ended in a point.

As it stepped forward and said, "Apologies, ma'am," whatever spell I'd fallen under broke and I realised there was actually this weird little creature standing in my room.

I jumped up, grabbing my umbrella and stepping forward. As I smacked it in the head, it kept talking. And no matter how much I hit it, it kept talking, taking each hit in stride.

"Yes, ma'am. I quite understand. However, I am here on behalf of my prince. After a week of making absolutely no headway with talking to you, Master Drake felt that it might be necessary–"

I froze, that name feeling too familiar. "Wait, what?"

It stood up straight, blinking its little black eyes rapidly as though used to hiding its true feelings. "Master Drake wished me to fetch you so the two of you can have a frank discussion."

The umbrella was still over my shoulder, ready to hit it again. "Master Drake?" I mused. "Drake. Why do I know that name?"

"He used to live next door to you, ma'am."

I involuntarily looked back to the picture still in my other hand.

"Yes, ma'am. The very same." There was a pause. "Sort of," it amended.

I looked back at the creature. "Drake's back?"

The creature nodded. "Yes, ma'am."

"And he sent…" I waved the umbrella in its direction. "You?"

"Truman, ma'am." It bowed.

My umbrella-wielding arm dropped by my side. "Truman? That's… That's you?"

"Yes, ma'am. It is a pleasure to make your acquaintance." It – he? – bowed again.

"And… Drake wants to talk to me?" Something wasn't making sense and I was feeling rather overwhelmed and confused.

"He's been trying to talk to you all week, ma'am."

I frowned. "What? How has he…?" I paused. "The new guy next door. Is that…?"

Truman nodded. "Yes, ma'am. He had hoped that you'd remember him and the whole process would go more smoothly. Since it has not, he sent me."

"Because that makes sense…" I muttered to myself.

"He's waiting for you, ma'am."

I looked at the picture again and then back to Truman. I had never seen nor heard of something like him existing ever. So, bet was I'd fallen asleep at my desk again, making this a dream and that meant it would be totally fine to go with him. If I wasn't asleep, Drake used to be my neighbour, and this little thing seemed totally harmless, so that made it totally fine to go with him. Right? Sure.

I tightened my grip on my umbrella and nodded. "Okay. I'll come now."

Truman smiled politely and inclined his head. "Might I suggest leaving the umbrella, ma'am?"

I put it down slowly. "Sure."

Truman inclined his head again and set off at a trot towards my bedroom door. I followed behind him, out of my house and over to the neighbours'. As we went, doors opened before him and closed behind me. I watched them carefully but decided it was best to just act like it was normal.

As we walked into the house, I looked around. It all looked the same as it had since they'd moved in twelve years earlier. But I was distracted when I heard a low mumbling and saw another little creature shuffling around.

I watched it carefully as it was lumbering around, a frown on its little features and its teeth bared.

"Um…how… How can I understand you?" I asked as it suddenly occurred to me.

"Hellspawn – the denizens of Hell – are built to speak and understand all languages, living and dead," Truman answered.

"Dead is relative," the other one said grumpily. "Plenty of use for dead languages down home." It looked up at me, licked the corner of his mouth quickly, and growled a little.

"Ma'am, meet Ignacio," Truman said as though we were just pretending that they hadn't mentioned Hell and that Ignacio was eyeing me off like he wanted to eat me.

There was a more frantic shuffling noise and I turned to see a third creature. This one was looking at me with great big, awed eyes. It was wearing a maid's apron and holding a big grey cat.

It stopped at my feet and held the cat up to me.

"Mr Muffin?" I wondered as the cat mewed up at me apathetically.

The cat didn't answer but the little creature did as it chattered up at me in a language made up of something like snarls and growls and yips. I of course couldn't understand it, but I got the feeling I was supposed to take the cat.

"Kyle said if you don't want to eat it, he'll be happy to," came a deep voice and I twisted to see the guy – Drake apparently – walk into the room.

I wasn't sure what to address first, but it seemed like a good idea to take the cat from Kyle in case he decided to eat me for refusing. That also delayed me thinking about how hot Drake was and kept my mind on the more pressing matters.

"Oh," I started slowly as I gently picked the cat out of Kyle's hands. "Um… Thanks. I'll save it for…later."

I smiled down at Kyle and, though he looked pleased, he also looked a little disappointed.

Drake chuckled and it sent a jolt of tingles across my skin. "Devilbums don't do flowers. This was the best he could come up with."

"This is Mrs Finster's cat!" I whispered to him, forgetting all my shyness and all thoughts of his naked abs in the face of the absolutely absurd situation I'd found myself in.

Drake smirked like he remembered Mrs Finster. "Then we'll take him back to her. Won't we, boys?" he asked them.

Kyle's face fell but he nodded and held his hands out for the cat again. I looked to Drake, who nodded reassuringly so I passed Mr Muffin back to Kyle.

"You put that back where you found it, Kyle!" Drake said, his voice a warning. "Ignacio, help him."

Ignacio muttered under his breath and started trying to usher Kyle out again. Kyle sighed then meandered out, sneaking looks back at me, carrying the oversized Mr Muffin comically in his tiny arms.

"He's been very excited to meet you," Drake explained.

I looked back to Drake and laughed, "What?"

My laughter died on my lips as Drake's lips tipped in a cocky half-smirk and his pale blue gaze raked over me. "He wasn't the only one. Although I have very different things in mind for our reunion."

I blushed as Truman cleared his throat. "I'll go and keep an eye on the others, sir."

Drake nodded, but didn't take his eyes off me. "Thank you, Truman."

I looked around the room, trying to think of anything to say that might diffuse the heat his gaze was eliciting in me. "Devilbums?" I finally said.

Drake's smile widened. "Devilbums."

"Why…?" I cleared my throat. "*What* are devilbums?"

"Think of the cherubim."

"Cherubim?"

"Big fat babies. Wings. Halo."

I nodded. "Right. Cherubim."

"The devilbums are Hell's version of them."

Because this was all making total sense. "Right. Of course."

Drake's chuckle was low and I could have sworn I felt it like a wave; emanating from him and washing over me with small vibrations. "Sit down. Be comfortable. Please."

I felt like I was on autopilot. My legs took me to a couch, but I was still just trying to get my head around what was happening.

"Uh. The–"

"Petersons?" Drake finished and I nodded. "They had the sudden urge to holiday in the Bahamas."

I nodded. "Of course, they did," I breathed as I looked around. "Truman… Truman said you want to talk to me?"

"That's what you want to start with?" Drake asked.

Honestly, I had too many questions to know where to start. So, I shrugged. "I don't… It seems as good as any."

Drake ran his hand over his chin as his eyes slid off me for a moment. "I get it. You haven't seen me for twelve years and suddenly I'm sending Truman over to talk to you."

"Truman called you a prince?"

Drake sighed as he looked back to me again. He nodded as he made himself comfortable in the giant armchair he somehow made look farcically small. "Prince with a lower case 'p', mind. Capital 'p' is something else entirely."

"I don't follow."

"Since I left, I've been living with my father. Things are…different there. They have their own ways of doing things. The short of it is, though, I need a wife."

He stopped talking, but I didn't say anything either. I wasn't sure if I was still processing it or waiting for him to continue – although I couldn't tell whether I wanted him to admit it was a joke or just give me some more information.

"You…need a wife?" I heard myself ask.

Drake nodded. "Yes."

Despite how insane it was, I had a feeling about where this was going. "So why did you want to talk to me?"

"Because why look for a wife when I already have one?"

5

Drake

She was understandably confused.

"You already have one?" she clarified, stiltedly. "A wife?"

My inflated ego heard a touch of jealousy in her voice and my smirk grew as I leant towards her. "Age means nothing in the afterlife, Serenity. We said our vows, twelve of your years ago, and I've come to collect my wife."

Okay. That might have taken it a little too far.

She blanched. But kudos to the human, she didn't get up and run away. Her eyes narrowed and her face contorted as she seemed to be trying to get her head around that. I watched her hand go to her mouth as she blinked rapidly. Then she lifted her hand away, opened her mouth, decided against it, and put her hand back. I could have read her mind, but it was more fun not knowing what was causing all those facial expressions, ranging from concern to acceptance, worry to relaxed, confused to resigned.

Finally, she took a deep breath, rearranged in her seat and folded her hands in her lap. "I'm sorry. You… You think I'm your wife and you're here to…collect me?"

I nodded. "Yes."

"Because your father…?" She breathed out heavily. "And you're a prince… If the devilbums are the cherubim of Hell, then…?" She looked at me abruptly and I saw the panic on her face.

"My father is the Lord of Hell. I am a prince of Hell and all hellspawn."

She swallowed hard. "And collect me? You want me to go to…?" She pointed down.

"Hell," I confirmed with a nod, despite the fact down wasn't really exact.

"Are you going to…kill me?" she squeaked and I found myself laughing roughly.

"No."

"Then how would I get–?"

"There are ways in without dying. You just have to know how to find them."

"Because we…we're married?" she whispered.

"Twelve years."

She was staring at me like she had no idea if I was insane, or what she should say next, or if maybe she was insane. She needed more proof than even the devilbums could give her. I could go with the big reveal, but that had the unintended consequence of making it look like we played for the other team. So, something else.

"Do you remember that day?" I asked her.

Her gaze focussed, but her teeth still had hold of her lip as her eyes narrowed. I watched her let go of her lip slowly as though it was coming back to her.

"I…think so…" she said slowly and I almost saw a hint of the girl I'd left behind in her eyes.

"Do you remember…" I started as I slowly brought my hand up, "what you had in your hand?"

She cocked her head as she watched my fingers rub together, and she gasped in delight when the little wilted daisy appeared in it with a brief flash of flame.

"You… Is that?"

I passed it to her and she took it tentatively. As she did, I looked around with pride as the field and creek spread out around us.

"Oh, my God…" she breathed as she spun around. One hand went to her mouth, in surprise this time, and those dazzling green eyes shone bright as she looked around. Her child-self ran through her and right over to me. "How did you…?"

"With absolutely no help from my grandfather, I assure you."

She looked at me and I could tell she'd at least stopped questioning my sanity…sort of.

"You… This is real?" She ran her hand through the grass then pulled her hand away quickly as she realised it was tangible. Her eyes snapped to me. "*Is* this real?"

I licked my lip. "Real is relative."

"How did you…?"

"I'm technically Nephilim, and I've got the power that comes with it."

"You're actually the son of the real devil? Like Bible shit, right now?"

"Not just the Bible. But yeah."

"Not just…" she breathed as she looked around some more.

I let it fade back to the Petersons' front room. "I just need a few days of your time."

"Wait. *You* made the Petersons move?"

I nodded. "I did."

"And you just made outside be inside."

My eyebrow rose of its own accord. "Kind of."

"Why don't you just make me go with you?" She frowned. "Can you just make me go with you?"

I scoffed. "Yeah, I could. I could make your parents be totally fine with it, too. But the men in my family find kidnapping a woman for a wife is a lot more hassle than it's worth. Not that my father really learned his lesson on that one."

"So…you need my…permission?"

"I don't *need* it. I'd prefer it."

"Why?"

I shrugged. There were a lot of reasons. "It makes the marriage claim more powerful."

"Why does your dad want you to marry now? Aren't you only…? What? Twenty-one?"

I nodded once as I stood up. "Yes–"

"Then why–?"

"–and no."

Her mouth closed as she seemed to rethink whatever it was she'd been about to say. Instead, she just looked at me in question.

I sighed. "We're not sharing backstories. Suffice to say that time works…differently down there. Which is why I only need you for a couple of days."

"Is that a couple of days here or there?"

"Here."

"How many days there?"

"As little as possible," I promised, my tone inadvertently curt.

She frowned at me again. "Excuse me?"

Like I had to explain myself to her. "What? It's a temporary arrangement. I don't want to spend more time with you than necessary."

All wonder was gone from her face and replaced with annoyance.

I wasn't a stranger to heat. I lived with it on a daily basis. Anger. Lust. Annoyance. Excitement. Fire. And this little human was making me feel the literal heat. I just had to work out how much of it was annoyance and how much was excitement.

"You send Truman into my room to ask me a favour, the least you could do is fake some humility," she said, crossing her arms.

"Firstly, I fake nothing. Secondly, I couldn't if I wanted to."

Her frown deepened. "What does that mean?"

"I am incapable of lying."

"But demons and stuff–"

"Are an entirely different breed. I'm half-angel. The rules apply. Mostly."

"Okay." She started pacing. "Let's pretend I believe this–"

"You want more pr–?"

"Shut up. Let me think." She paused long enough in her pacing to check I was going to be quiet. I was going to be quiet. "Say I believe all this. You want me to go with you to Hell as your wife? You said just for a couple of days. That's all you want? Why?"

"I just need to show Dad and Hell I've got a wife, that you are she, and have it all signed off. Then I can send you home and we can both go back to our lives."

She blinked. "This is a *really* inappropriate time. I have exams in a couple of weeks." She stopped and I practically saw the lightbulb go off. "Wait. Time works differently?"

"Yes."

"As in, people here would experience two days and I could experience…?"

"As little as possible," I reassured her, not wanting to risk her saying no.

"When you say as little time as possible…how *long* could that feasibly be?"

What? I felt like I could see where this was going now, and I refused to believe my wife was such a nerd. "You're considering my offer so you have more study time?"

She shrugged. "Just more time really. It's my eighteenth birthday next week. My uni application choices were a total disaster – seriously, why not a single Arts degree? Exams are coming up soon. Then school's over. Forever. Who's ready for that? A…pause could be just what I need."

"Let me get this straight. You're considering willingly entering Hell as a vacation?"

"Does the devil make a habit of torturing his daughter-in-law?"

I was pretty sure I'd underestimated her. And I didn't hate it. She definitely wasn't the little girl I'd left behind. She was more. "It honestly depends on your definition of torture."

"A normal person's definition of torture!" she cried, flailing her arms.

I rubbed the back of my head. "Yeah, there isn't really a *normal* definition."

"Sir, Mrs Finster's cat has been returned to its squishy cushion."

I turned to see Truman and the boys standing at the side of the room.

"She coming home?" Kyle asked, using the language of Hell in his shyness.

"I'm just about to work that out," I told him in kind.

"Sorry. What was that?" she asked.

I gave her my most sinful crooked smile, and switched back to English. "Kyle wants to know if you're coming home with us?"

She breathed out heavily. "I have to be dreaming," she muttered. "Or mad. Or both." Another deep breath and she pinned me with that green gaze. "When are you going?"

"We're all leaving tonight."

Another frown at what was realistically little more than a polite order. "And if I choose not to go?"

I turned one of my fierce stares on her. "We're *all* leaving tonight."

She blinked in surprise and I snuck a peak into her mind.

Oh, it's going to be like that, is it?

He is super hot, though.

That is not a good reason.

Is a bad reason, though?

Fine. I'm going. I'm going.

If he's going to take me anyway, I may as well choose it.

"Fine. I'll agree to come. But you have to tell my parents."

I'd faced the most evil beings in creation. I'd fought and beaten every single one of them except my father. What were two human parents compared to that?

And the sooner my wife was in Hell, the sooner the job was done and I could shed this ridiculous humanity.

6

Wren

So, I was going to Hell. Literally for once, as opposed to all the times Harmony and I had said it about one of our jokes. Because what was agreeing to go to Hell? I mean that was everyone's usual Friday, wasn't it?

Drake and the devilbums followed me back to our house. Well, I say followed. Kyle ran ahead, plastering himself against the door as though he couldn't wait to go inside.

"Mum! Dad!" I called as I walked in, narrowly avoiding being run over by Kyle in his excitement to run inside and investigate things.

"What?" Dad called and Mum replied, "In here."

I had no idea how to even begin to broach this. But sitting down seemed like a good start. "Can you guys come to the living room, please?"

"Don't try having a family meeting without me," Tilly called, because of course the *whole* family was home, then I heard her thundering down the stairs. The thundering stopped and I heard her say, "Oh, my."

I looked up and saw she was staring at Drake. So much so, she hadn't noticed the devilbums until Ignacio snuffled up the stairs to sniff her.

"Oh, my God! What is that?" Tilly screamed.

"What? What's wrong?" Mum asked as she came running in.

Dad wasn't far behind her. All three of them were standing at the edges of the living room and staring between Drake and the devilbums. Truman stood patiently by Drake's leg. Ignacio was still sniffling about suspiciously. And Kyle was investigating everything, mostly with his tongue.

"Guys, this is Drake," I started. "He and his mum used to live next door."

Mum waved absently. Dad's jaw dropped. And Tilly had pulled herself together enough to bat her eyelashes at him.

"And…these are Truman, Ignacio and Kyle…" I continued, pointing to each of them.

Another absent wave. Some more slack-jaw. And a little fright.

"Can we all sit down?" I asked. "Drake has a…favour to ask you guys."

"A favour?" Dad asked as the three of them did much like I'd recently done, and auto-piloted their way to sitting down.

I nodded. "Yeah. So, funny story. Drake needs me to pop down to Hell for the weekend."

I watched all three of them look to at least one devilbum.

"Hell?" Dad asked.

"For the weekend?" Mum added.

I motioned for Drake to sit and also sat. "Yeah. See, the thing is Drake's dad is – like – the real devil and–"

There was a clattering noise above me.

"Kyle!" Drake hissed with a forced chuckle.

Mum, Dad, Tilly and I all followed his gaze and I saw Kyle swinging upside down on the chandelier with a big goofy smile on his read, leathery face. As much as Ignacio freaked me out, Kyle was like a puppy I just wanted to look after.

When I looked back to Drake, he chuckled roughly. "Excuse him. Even Hell hasn't found a way to beat the optimism out of him."

"Oh no." Kyle shook his head, his bat ears flapping madly. "They tried."

"Sir, should we get on with it?" Truman asked.

I didn't wonder where Ignacio was. I was afraid to see what he was up to.

Drake cleared his head and edged forwards on his seat, towards my parents. "Look, I know this is all rather unorthodox–"

Truman cleared his throat. "Religion, sir."

Drake sighed. "Right. I know this is…weird."

"You're really the little boy from next door?" Mum asked, looking him over.

"Yeah." Drake scoffed. "All grown up."

"How's your mother?" Dad asked.

"Dead," Drake said simply.

"Oh."

Drake gave a single nod. "Look, all I'm asking it to borrow Serenity for…I'm not exactly sure how the time difference works. But – like – the weekend at most. I think."

"You want to…borrow our daughter?" Mum asked.

Drake sighed again. "My dad–"

"The actual devil?" Dad clarified.

"Yeah, him. He wants me to find a wife."

"A wife?" Tilly asked.

"Yep. I need to get married–"

"To *her*?" Trust my sister to find the least plausible part of this whole thing was Drake wanting me.

Drake cocked his head. "Ah. Well, this is where things get simpler. We're already married–"

"WHAT?" Mum, Dad and Tilly cried.

I took a deep breath. "Not like that. You remember that stupid little ceremony we did down the creek in the back yard when I was – like – five?"

Tilly snorted. "You mean the one you've kept the photo of all these years, and you and your friends dream about Drake coming back and marrying you for real?"

My cheeks heated and I just caught Drake's self-satisfied smirk before I looked down quickly in an effort to hide my shame.

"Convenient thing is, it counts," Drake said.

"That counts?" Dad asked, panicking.

"Not by human law," Drake said quickly. "But when the rules of Heaven and Hell were being set up, things were a lot…simpler."

"So, by the laws of…?" Mum started.

"My father." Drake nodded.

"The two of you are married?"

Drake shrugged unapologetically. "Counts. I just need to take her home, show her off a little, make Dad happy, and send her back home."

"You want to take our daughter to Hell?" Dad asked.

Now that I had it all sorted out in my head, this circular discussion was a total pain in the arse. I licked my lips and leant towards Drake. "You know how you said you could make them…?"

He nodded. "Yeah?"

"Did you mean it?"

"Yeah."

I nodded as I sat back and smiled at my family. "Great. Do that and let's go."

I'd surprised him. "You want me to…?"

"Yeah," I answered.

He shrugged. "Sure. Can do."

I stood up, ignoring my parents' looks of confusion. "I'm going to pack a bag."

"Why?" Drake asked.

I looked at him as witheringly as I was capable. "So, I have stuff to wear."

"I can make your parents not worry about you disappearing for a few days. You think you need to bring things with you?"

"Are your powers like unlimited or something?"

"Or something."

"So, you just do whatever you want?"

He sighed. "Just do what you need to do. I'll be here."

"Kyle help?" Kyle squeaked, throwing himself off the chandelier.

Ignacio appeared seemingly out of nowhere and tried to catch him. They both ended up in a pile of red leather and brown fur on the floor.

"You guys okay?" I asked and Ignacio gave what appeared to be his usual string of intelligible mutterings.

"Kyle help!" Kyle repeated, hauling himself up and running up the stairs as fast as his little legs would carry him.

I followed him and noticed Truman followed me. Ignacio growled when I looked back, but stayed with Drake and my parents. As I walked into my room, I heard them having a conversation about the weather in Hell and I assumed Drake had deployed his mojo to make them all okay with it.

In all honesty, I wasn't sure how okay I was with it. But it seemed like a better idea to at least pretend I had a choice in the matter and had chosen to go to Hell with a guy claiming I was his wife, rather than be kidnapped. Who knew what would happen if I hadn't gone willingly?

Before I could change my mind, I packed a duffel bag with some essentials, some school books, and some toiletries. Truman had this stoic presence that weirdly gave me a huge sense of comfort. He just stood and watched like some sort of soothing security guard. Kyle wasn't a lot of use, but I didn't mind him so much. He kept picking things up and asking what they were, often holding them right up to his eye or shoving them in his mouth for a good old taste.

"Why is it I can understand you now?" I asked him.

"Serenity coming home. Serenity Master Drake's. Serenity understand now."

Well, no. Serenity didn't understand now. But he seemed pretty happy with his explanation so I looked at Truman. He wasn't a lot of help either, with nothing but an inclined head, so I made a mental note to ask Drake later.

I batted Kyle's head out of my bag gently, and zipped it up. There was a moment where I managed to get Truman covering Kyle's eyes to let me get changed – couldn't very well got to Hell in my school uniform – without either of them looking. And by the time we got back downstairs, my family seemed perfectly happy to see me go.

"You have a wonderful time," Mum said.

Tilly looked at Drake out of the corner of her eyes. "You have a *really* wonderful time."

I laughed and nudged her. "Funny."

"Be safe," Dad said. "And we'll see you in a few days."

I didn't think I'd remind him I was going to Hell in case that ruined the spell or whatever it was that was making them happy. It certainly made it easier for them to accept my choice, such as it was.

"Ready?" Drake asked.

I nodded.

"Boys."

The devilbums all crowded around Drake's legs and Truman looked up at me.

"Best hold tight, ma'am."

I looked up at Drake and he gave a single nod. I shuffled as close to him as I could get and he put one unnecessarily strong arm around me, pulling me even closer so I had a singular view of his chest. I grabbed hold of the front of his t-shirt with absolutely no idea what was about to happen.

I blinked and was still waiting.

Then Drake let go of me and I looked around.

We weren't in my parents' hallway anymore. We were at the edge of what looked like a forest, a crumbling path under foot. Chill wind buffeted me as Drake stepped away, heading for a large rock. The devilbums followed him. Truman trotting rather stately. Ignacio in a sort of hunched over ramble. And Kyle bounding around and covering twice as much ground as he needed to.

I pulled my bag strap further up my shoulder and hurried to catch up with Drake's effortless, long strides.

Around a slight bend was a cave. We all entered and I was just wondering how far we were going to go when I realised the rock had turned from grey to a red-brown and the temperature had risen significantly.

"Welcome to Hell, ma'am," Truman said, looking back at me.

"We're...here?"

Kyle nodded as he went running ahead. "Came in the backdoor."

I looked around as the tunnel started to get more occupied. Big, round demon-looking creatures with helmets and pikes. Other devilbums running around quickly through everything, even one with an executioner mask on. Some demons were dragging people around with them, people who looked at me with the utter resigned subjugation of those who'd lived it for literal eternity. The whole atmosphere was oppressive. And the heat. I thought Australia in the middle of summer was oppressive, unrelenting heat. It wore away at your will and exhausted you. This was somehow worse. And the sounds. Sounds were reaching my ears, and getting louder by the step. It took me longer than it should have to recognise what they were.

I swallowed. "Is that... Are they screams?"

"There aren't any fluffy clouds down here, Serenity," Drake said. "Eternal torment around the clock for eternity."

I wasn't sure what to say to that, but it went a ways to explaining his personality. If I'd been surrounded by all this for years, I'd be pretty cranky too.

A group of devilbums scurried towards us with wild jabbers, and I pressed myself against the wall to avoid them. Kyle jabbered back, shaking his fist, as they passed. I took a deep breath, but gave Kyle the best smile I could when he turned a grin on me.

I followed Drake and the devilbums through the tunnels of Hell, feeling more and more astounded. There were a seemingly endless torrent of demons and people and so many random doors behind which screams of all varieties could be heard. Some of them made my skin crawl, some sent nervous tingles down my spine, some made my hair stand on end. But they were all, undeniably, horrific.

Drake finally stopped in a seemingly non-descript tunnel and pushed open a door.

Kyle went scampering in and immediately started exploring.

Ignacio stalked in, sniffing the air.

Truman peered around Drake, but held back from entering.

It was like none of them had seen the room before.

Interested, I took in everything I could from the tunnel. I could see the pattern of flame flickering, sending shadows dancing across the little I could see. There was the end of a four-poster bed covered in what looked like a plush comforter. There was the back of a chair, a whole lot of floor space and an apparent lack of windows. Which, I realised, shouldn't really surprise me given where I was.

"Are you going in?" Drake asked and I looked to see him watching me with expectant annoyance.

I pulled myself together, nodded, and awkwardly squeezed between him and the door frame to enter the room. My body pressed up right against his, not that he seemed to mind in the slightest. I hoped my red cheeks could be attributed to the unnecessary heat and not a sign I was embarrassed I'd somewhat enjoyed it. I cleared my throat and took another look around the room.

Lack of windows notwithstanding, it didn't exactly scream Hell.

In fact, it was almost cosy.

As I looked around, the fire in the hearth grew and candles flickered to life, giving me a better view of the dark wood-panelled walls, the furniture made of a mixture of lighter wood and stone, the materials in red and brown and off-white, and the polished stone floor. It reminded me of ski chalets you saw in movies, although I was sure the fireplace was unnecessary.

"This is…" I breathed out.

"It is the best Hell has to offer," Truman said as though it was an apology.

I looked at him with a small smile. "I was going to say kind of nice." I walked towards the bed and put my bag down.

"Don't leave this room without me or one of the boys," Drake commanded as I unzipped to unpack.

"So, I don't get my own devilbums?" I rolled my eyes as I pulled off my hoody.

"Truman, Ignacio and Kyle will see to every need…I cannot." Somehow, he managed to make that sound super dirty and sexy at the same time it sounded incredibly domineering – and not just in a good way.

"Great. And where's your room?"

There was a long enough pause that I knew I wasn't going to like his next sentence.

Finally, he confirmed all my suspicions. "This is *our* room."

Drake

"You have to be kidding me," she said, crossing her arms and turning back to me with a glare that could freeze the molten throne under Dad's arse.

"Yeah, I don't do that," I told her.

"I am *not* sharing a room with you."

"You don't really have a choice."

"You never mentioned I'd have to share a room with you."

"We're married. What did you expect?"

"I'm going home."

"I'm not taking you."

"I'm sure I can find my own way out."

She walked towards the door, but I put my hand against the frame of the closed door to stop her opening it.

"Serenity, you go wandering around out there and who knows how long you'll be lost."

"Wren."

I blinked. "What?"

"I go by Wren now."

I huffed. "Fine. Wren."

She was a holy enigma and I couldn't get my head around it. By human standards, she was taking this far better than I'd expected. I'd even seen her smiling absently as she watched Kyle's antics. She'd barely baulked at the idea of being my wife and coming to Hell. But sharing a room with me was enough to break the deal? I didn't understand. And I sure as Heaven wasn't about to negotiate anything. She was in my domain now with no way home; I was in charge now. Although, I had to concede that I wanted this to go better than it currently was.

She was centimetres from me, smelling sweet and tempting. She was glaring at me, which got every single motor I owned running – nothing I liked better than angry sex. And my wife wasn't just angry with me, she was exuding hatred in a way that made me hard. My fingers itched to see if she was as soft as she looked. I wanted to know if she tasted as sweet as she smelled. I wanted to know if that streak of vixen I'd seen behind the mask of innocence would take over in bed.

But it was more than that.

As her green eyes bored into mine, I felt the first real battle of wills I'd encountered since I'd arrived in Hell. I clashed with my father constantly, but nothing I did would diminish his supremacy over me and Hell. I could pick a fight all I liked with any other hellspawn but, no matter what I told them, they always deferred to me. I'd been caught between being more powerful than all but one man for eons, but Wren didn't care about propriety.

And that sent a thrill through me I'd never felt before.

"We are *not* sharing a room," she said through gritted teeth.

"This is not a negotiation. That bed is our–"

The door pushed me forwards, which meant I ran into Wren. My arms went around her instinctively to keep her from falling. For a brief moment, there was less hatred in her eyes and I saw there was a flicker of desire. She wanted me. Even if she didn't want to. That I could work with. The rules of Hell were not the rules of Heaven or Earth.

"Um, sir?" I heard and remembered why Wren was in my arms.

I let her go somewhat abruptly and turned to the guard demon. "What is it, Neville?" I snapped.

Neville bowed his head. "Sorry to interrupt, sir. But his devilness is ready for you."

I sighed and prayed to Grandad for strength – someone in our family had to be normal, surely? "Right. He wants us now then?"

"Yes, sir. He's got a whole…thing in motion."

Of course, he did. He'd regaled me with many plans before I'd left. They'd all included dinner and at least one show. "Sure." I looked to the boys. "Truman, unpack Wren's things."

Wren started, "I can–"

But I cut her off. "This could take hours. In the best-case scenario. Truman will unpack your things." I looked her over in her jeans and t-shirt. "How confident are you in meeting the devil wearing that?"

She looked down at herself. "Is there something wrong with what I'm wearing?"

I snapped my mouth shut before something unnecessarily rude came out. "I don't care what you wear. Dad will have a problem with whatever you wear. So, it's up to you."

Wren huffed out. "So helpful. Okay. I'm fine then."

"Neville, take us to my father," I said.

He bowed and turned to lead us out.

"Kyle come?"

I looked back at him as Wren followed Neville. Ignacio had one hand firmly around Kyle's arm to stop him following, and Kyle's face was turned down in an epic pout, even by his standards.

"Not this time. Stay and help Truman." Kyle's frown turned upside down and he wrenched himself out of Ignacio's grip to run to Wren's bag. "Help, Kyle! I said help. Don't break–"

Wren stopped me with a soft hand on my arm. "You put the things back where you think I'd put them," she said to Kyle gently. Kyle's head tilted sideways. "You remember where I got them all from?" Kyle nodded. "Okay. You put them back in the most similar places. Yeah?"

He nodded. "Kyle do that."

I wasn't sure what surprised me more. Wren's hand on me – such a simple, even almost tender, unconscious action – or how kind she already was with Kyle.

Kyle was young by devilbum norms. He wasn't so much simple as he was enthusiastic and loyal, and still incredibly naïve.

"Do as Wren says," I snapped before sweeping out after Neville.

It's not like I needed him to show me the way. But something about it felt more official than if I'd just taken Wren myself. Plus, she'd taken me off guard one too many times in as many minutes, and I felt all weird and more annoyed than usual.

Wren kept up pretty well through the tunnels. I'm sure she paid more attention to who – or what – we passed than I did. I was just focussed on the doors to my father's throne room, seeing them in my mind's eye long before they actually appeared in view.

Neville stopped just short of them.

The doors burst open before we got to them and heat blasted out along with the familiar sound of the bongo introduction to Dad's favourite Earth song. My dad was nothing if not a showman.

"Son, you have returned," his voice boomed ominously around the room as we stepped into it.

I could feel Wren trembling next to me and that pissed me off more than his melodrama.

"Shut off the theatrics, old man," I yelled.

The smoke condensed and solidified into the image of my...

"Oh, come off it," I muttered, looking him over. I crossed my arms and waited to see what he was going to do with this.

He was red from head to toe, his dark hair slicked back, horns protruding proudly, his pinstripe suit impeccable, his Oxfords polished, his cane shiny, his grin white, even the beard on his chin was pointed to perfection.

And he was going to do nothing with this because he had to put on The Show; most newbies to Hell got it – flames and heat and death. You know, the postcard stuff. He'd even strung up some souls around the room so they looked properly tormented. I saw Larry among them and nodded to him. I saw a thin flicker of a grin cross his gaunt, dark, gormless features and then he was back to acting again.

I put a hand behind Wren and she took a few stumbling steps towards my father. "Wren, allow me to introduce the Lord of Hell. Lucifer. Satan. Hades. The Devil. I call him Dad. Dad, this is my wife, Serenity."

"Most men seem happier on their wedding days," Dad said to Wren in a mock-whisper as he leant towards her and I didn't blame the freaked out look she shot me.

"Yeah, thanks," I told him. "Most married men presumably *want* to be married and aren't stuck in a timeless hell."

"Cheery lad, isn't he? Gets it from his mother's side," Dad said as he waggled his eyebrows and Wren's look was a little more 'is he for real?' this time.

"Are we doing this dinner, or what?" I snapped.

Dad sighed in exasperation and waved his fingers. "All right, everyone. Show's over." The tortured souls were released from their manacles to go be tortured somewhere else, the temperature fell to its usual level of uncomfortably hot, and the room returned to the usual dark stone chamber with the throne at one end. The dining table currently running down it was a special feature.

"All right, Drake," Larry nodded as he floated over.

"Yeah, all right, Larry," I replied. "How's it going?"

"Oh, you know. Nice to get out for a bit. You know? Do something a little different."

I nodded. "I'll bet."

"We still on for tomorrow?"

"Yeah. I'll see you then."

"See you later." He floated a little towards Wren. "Nice to meet you, Mrs Drake."

Wren's already pale face lost another level of colour as she nodded slowly. "Uh, you, too… Larry, was it?"

"Out of the flesh, ma'am."

"Larry, don't you have somewhere to be?" Dad called.

Larry threw me a grin. "See you later, then."

"Yeah. Later, Larry." I kicked my chin at him and he followed the rest of the souls up through the ceiling.

"This is…" Wren started. She licked her lip, then looked around me to Dad. "That's your… The Devil?"

I shrugged. "Yep." I strode towards Dad. "So, where's the step-monster?" In my case, it was true.

"Pleasure as always, Drake," came the hiss that signalled Esther and I heard Wren yelp.

I turned and gave Esther my fakest smile. "Looking terrifying as always," I told her.

Which wasn't a lie. Esther looked like she was carved from the purest white marble. Her skin and her hair were more suited to a winter wonderland than the fiery depths of the most condemned place in creation. She even wore all white clothes, not that they really covered anything. Her eyes were pure black. The only colour on her was red. Blood red. Her lips were red, her eyes were surrounded in red like a toddler had gone crazy with eye shadow, and she wore a red crown on her head. There were also the light splatters of blood constantly dripping over her body like she'd just come from a light shower.

"Thank you, Drake. This is your chosen wife?"

Esther's voice didn't grate on your ears, it wasn't even screeching. But every time she opened her mouth, I felt the same unpleasant shiver as when you hear fingernails scraping down a chalkboard.

"Wren, this is my father's wife, Esther." I pointed between the two of them.

Wren's eyes looked like they were about to bug out of her head as Esther glided towards her.

"Leave the human be," Dad snapped. "I worked *so* hard on this dinner. And I will not have it ruined because my family can't keep their teeth – or anything else – in their trousers. Do you hear me?" He lost the petulant child look and smiled at Wren. "Come, Serenity. Come and sit. Can I get you a drink?"

I watched Wren nod and move towards him like she was on autopilot. The first time I'd seen that behaviour, I'd failed to realise how fast her mind was whirring. I'd assumed it had slowed. I wasn't going to make that mistake with her again.

I took a quick dip into her mind and caught too many thoughts for even me to process. But she was processing it all in her own way and I was sure I'd see the girl who didn't shy away from challenging me again soon. I was mainly looking forward to seeing if she'd give challenging my father a shot, too.

"Excellent! Excellent," Dad exclaimed as he helped Wren into a seat to the left of the head of the table.

Esther made her creepy noiseless way to her chair at what I called the butt of the table – the opposite end to the head – and I dropped to Dad's right.

Dad waved his hands in a flourish I could see was becoming more astounding than confusing to Wren, and a flagon of wine appeared in his hand. I sighed loudly and Dad glared at me to be quiet.

"What?" I shook my head. "It's not even that good."

Dad gasped. "Not that…? How dare you! This was Alexander's favourite wine!"

I rolled my eyes. "Yeah. Still not that good."

"I'm sorry…" Wren said quietly, as though she was already regretting speaking. "Who is…Alexander?"

"Who is Alexander?" Dad asked, scoffing at me. "Alexander the Great!" Wren's face was still blank. "King of Macedon." Still blank. "His empire stretched from Greece to India, and down into Egypt."

Wren shrugged. "Don't know him."

Dad waved a hand at her. "Never mind. I'll introduce you to him later. He's wonderful at parties. But this," he held the jug aloft, "was his favourite wine."

"Little bit meaningless if she doesn't know who he is, don't you think?" I asked.

"No one asked you for your opinion, Mr Cranky-Pants." Dad looked at Wren. "Honestly. The boy's married, and he chooses to gripe over wine!" Dad laughed as he started pouring.

"Uh…I'm not quite…" Wren started uncertainly.

"Legal?" Dad clarified with a knowing wink and Wren nodded. "A concept that is *very* young in our world, darling."

"Oh."

"Besides, let's not pretend you haven't had a few drinks anyway, eh?" he chuckled as he sashayed over to me.

Wren said nothing, only blushed and took a sip of wine.

But she didn't need to, Dad made plenty of conversation for all of us. He talked through finishing with the wine, dinner appearing, the first two courses, and the intervening musical numbers, including a fire-juggling guard demon on a unicycle.

"Right. So, did you spend all week in bed?" Dad asked during the third course like it was normal dinner conversation. "Or did you show Drake around Earth for a bit, too?"

Wren choked on her mouthful. "Sorry?"

"Bed. Sex." Dad looked at her like he was sure she wasn't that stupid. Then he looked at Esther with an expectant hand flourish. "Am I speaking Greek?"

Esther's face was somehow expressionless and smug. "She understood you. He has failed to bed her."

I resented that. "Hang on—"

"Is this true, son?" Dad asked.

Wren was looking between everyone like she didn't want to believe the conclusion she'd come to.

"Yes," I finally admitted, somewhat sourly. "I haven't…bedded her."

Dad dropped his cutlery on his plate with a disappointed huff. "Well that doesn't count then."

"Excuse me?" Wren and I both asked.

Dad threw his arms up. "Doesn't count." He motioned between us. "Marriage only counts if you've consummated it."

"I'm not having sex with him!" Wren cried.

I wasn't sure what slight I wanted to address first. I pointed at Dad. "Firstly, you never said anything about me having to fuck her." I turned my finger on Wren. "Secondly, why not?"

Wren shook her head, dropped her cutlery onto her plate, and pushed herself to standing. "No. I'm not sleeping with a guy I've just met, let alone the son of the devil."

Dad sat forward and dropped every ounce of joviality he usually possessed. "You are here as Drake's wife, Serenity. You will not leave here until he has bedded you. You can fight all you like, but I always find these things are so much more…pleasurable when you just accept them."

Wren looked right at me with a scared determination on her face. "I'm not sleeping with you." She nodded as though she needed the encouragement, then looked at my father. "Thank you for dinner. It was…nice to meet you." She nodded once more, then hurried back out of the room.

"You are not going after her?" Esther asked, her voice as emotionless as always.

I shook my head. "I think it's safer I give her a moment. Neville'll show her back."

Dad's chuckle was soft and low, truly the devil the world thought they knew. "Well."

With one hand flourish, the dinner things were cleared away and there was a brandy balloon in front of the two of us. He picked his up and a cigar appeared in his other hand as he brought it to his lips, the tip burning bright as he inhaled. Esther disappeared, knowing she wasn't required and not wanting to be around my father longer than necessary.

"She's fun," Dad said slowly around the cigar, smoke billowing from his mouth. "I don't know if I should congratulate your choice of wife, or rebuke it."

I sighed as I downed the brandy in one gulp. Then again as the glass refilled itself automatically. "It seemed a good idea at the time."

"You thought it would be easier," he chided softly, as fatherly as he ever got.

I downed my glass again. "I did."

"It may yet come right."

"It might blow up in my face."

Through the smoke amassing around his face, all I could see was his devilish grin and the red glow of his eyes. "Either way, we ought to have a little fun."

"Easy for you to say," I muttered.

We sat in a semi-companionable semi-silence for the space of a few more drinks before I got up and went to see if my wife had calmed down.

8
Wren

I wasn't in Hell; I was in a madhouse. Had to be. No other sensible explanation.

Except the ridiculously incessant heat.

And the very realistic wails of the tortured constantly ringing in my ears like background noise at that point.

And the actual devil who'd managed to scare the pants off me just being in the same room as him even when he was being all…him.

And the devil's wife who would be the thing haunting my nightmares for the rest of my life.

Aside from that, and the very real feeling I had about everything, I could hardly believe I was in actual Hell. The devil was…flamboyant? That was the best word I had for it. He was flamboyant and extravagant, all at once amazing, ridiculous and terrifying. I couldn't get my head around it. But as antithetical as it seemed, that was the main reason I knew I wasn't mad; my brain never would have made up that sort of devil. It would just have been fire and death and fear.

While I'd been pretty scared since I arrived, I was mainly pissed off. The heat wasn't helping me keep a cool head, but mainly it was Drake. Being someone's wife was one thing

– a weird thing, true – but having to sleep with him before I could go home? No.

I wasn't going to be having sex with him. Ever.

So, my only other choice was to settle in for the foreseeable future and make myself at home. Which I did as best as I was able, all while Drake and I ignored each other like we were arguing ten-year-olds. He slept beside me, but other than that we spent no time together past as long as it took him to get into bed and get back out again.

"Truman?" I asked the devilbum about a week later as he tidied up around me.

"Yes, ma'am? Can I get you another book? Perhaps a snack?"

I shook my head with a smile. "No, thanks. I was just wondering if I could ask you a question."

"Anything, ma'am. We are here at your service."

Well, that was certainly true of Truman. Kyle and Ignacio though? Ignacio was barely visible, choosing to go stalking after Drake all day like he was a simulacrum of Drake's mood. And Kyle spent most of his time curled up, sleeping on the ottoman next to my feet, like some deformed yet still super adorable cat, while I read. Truman though was almost human in his behaviour and he was still a calming, comforting presence in my life. I felt like I could talk to him and he wouldn't think me stupid or idiotic or judge me.

"The whole time difference thing. How does it work?"

"How do you mean, ma'am?"

"Well, Drake mentioned time passes differently here…?"

Truman nodded. "It does."

"How?"

"Well, the opposite of Faery."

I blinked. "Of what?"

"Faery. Where the fae live."

"I... Obviously." I cleared my throat, putting a pin in that tangent. "But how does it work?"

"Time here moves faster than it does on Earth. So, you could experience many hundreds of years in the same time your family experience two days."

I swallowed. "Hundreds of years?"

He nodded. "Indeed, ma'am."

"And Drake's been here for...twelve years..."

"Millenia by our count, ma'am."

"But he stopped aging then?"

"Of course, ma'am." Truman chuckled. "Master Drake's immortal."

"But what about me?"

Truman looked at me. "You won't age while you're here, ma'am."

"Why not?"

Truman shuffled his feet a bit like he was uncomfortable. "You are...of age, ma'am. Biologically, there is no reason for you to age any more. Thus, you are...frozen, as it were."

I fanned myself. "God, if only," I laughed. "How serious is...Drake's dad about me not going home until we've had sex?"

"Deadly, ma'am. If you'll forgive the term. But his lordship is nothing if not stubborn. One of the many things Master Drake inherited from his father."

I sat back in the chair again and sighed, thinking.

If time moved that much differently, then I didn't have anything to worry about in terms of missing time on Earth. I could hold up the sex-embargo until...well, almost the end of time. All I had to do was wear down Drake's patience.

Once he decided I wasn't worth it, he'd take me home and find another wife. It wasn't going to be that difficult to find someone to sleep with him.

I'd thought about it.

Boy, had I thought about it.

I'd thought about it when I thought he was just a slightly over-eager if not creeper neighbour. Now that we were sharing a room? My imagination went into overdrive regularly. The fact I knew it was expected only made it worse. I asked myself so many times why I bothered resisting, because there was a part of me who would be very unopposed to sleeping with him. There was no down side really; sleep with him, probably have an *amazing* time, then go home. So why was I resisting?

I heard the door open and quickly pulled my book in front of my face.

"How was your day, sir?" Truman asked.

Drake grunted in reply.

"That well, sir? Excellent news. Do you want to shower, or—"

I snuck a look over the top of my book as Truman stopped speaking and saw Drake had pulled his top off. He was standing in nothing but his jeans and sneakers. His back muscles shifted under his glistening skin as he stretched and breathed out heavily. And that was enough to have me drooling, but when he turned around?

His body tapered to a sinful V, disappearing under the waistband of his pants. He was made out of rock-hard abs and strong arms, and my eyes always darted to the front of his jeans, sure I could make out the outline of his package. He looked barely a day over eighteen, but that body made me believe he'd been working on it for centuries.

It's not like I hadn't seen it all already. But every time was like the first time.

My eyes slid up and I saw him watching me. Talk about sinful.

If the previous week had made me believe anything, it was that Drake was Satan's son, because the boy was made for sin. It was like his natural default. Sin or anger. There was no in between.

"Are you reconsidering?" he asked me, his voice was low and rumbly, and made my stomach do funny things.

"No. I'm not," I told him in a huff as I forced my eyes back onto my book.

"How unfortunate. We won't have an excuse for being late then."

I looked up. "Late?"

He nodded as he unabashedly pulled his jeans off, leaving him naked. He stayed facing me long enough to give me plenty to ogle, obviously very proud when I didn't look away. It was partly a point of my own pride. It was also just because I liked the view. His arse was just as nice to ogle.

"Dad's decided on a party."

"A party?"

"Has a single week in Hell rendered you simple?" he huffed, moving through to the bathroom I was sure was only there for my benefit.

I looked at Truman for a moment, debating the sense in following him to continue the conversation. Truman gave me a look that quite clearly told me I had to make my own decisions.

"Yes. Well, we've seen where that gets me," I muttered testily as I dropped the book and hopped up anyway.

Drake was in the shower, which I was pretty sure was also only for my benefit. It was such a perfect set up that I suspected someone was using their powers. The steam swirled up around his legs and lower body, embracing him and making the scene sexy by what it hid as much as the glimpses it showed.

"I'm perfectly fine, thank you," I told him.

"I can see that."

He looked at me over his shoulder, those blue eyes smouldering as they traced over my body. Warmth spread across my skin like a caress and I didn't know if he was doing that or if I was doing it all by myself. In the privacy of my mind, I let myself revel in the feeling of being wanted, of being desired, of what his desire did to me. But in the public of my face, I frowned.

"I meant my head's fine."

"You've just wanted to be a parrot since you were a little girl?"

I leant against the door frame and frowned harder. "Very funny."

"I seem to remember you wanting to be a mermaid."

I pushed myself off the door and stomped closer to him, not sure what I was going to do but there I was. "I'm terribly sorry so much of this is incredibly confusing to me, Drake. I'll just magically know everything like you do and then you won't even have to talk to me, shall I?"

The corner of his lip tipped up as he stepped to stand right in front of me. "You join me and we certainly won't have to talk."

I pushed him in the chest and he obligingly took a couple of steps backwards even though I never would have had the strength to move him if he hadn't wanted me to. I ignored how warm and soft his skin had felt. To very little success. "I'm not joining you."

"You just wanted an excuse to look a little longer?"

"I wanted to know what you meant about your dad's party!" I cried, very close to losing my dignity, my sanity, and my clothes. I took a step back. "And if there was more to why you wanted an excuse to be late."

"Getting you in bed not a good enough excuse for you?" he asked, frowning at me.

"I've been here a week. I've noticed things–"

"Oh, yeah?" he interrupted me, turning the taps off. "What do you think you've noticed, human?"

I wasn't going to lose my bluster in front of him. If I was going to survive this, I had to stay strong. "It doesn't take a genius to work out you and your dad don't get on. Something tells me you'd be happy with any excuse to avoid a party of his."

His eyes raked over me, a red glow burning in the depths of them, but not quite taking over yet. "Are you offering me an excuse?" his voice had a hint of growly to it. I just couldn't tell if lust or anger was taking him over this time.

I shook myself out as I nodded. "Maybe."

He took enough slow steps towards me to be standing right in front of me again. "One night – or day – in my bed and you can go home," he purred, the red getting stronger in his eyes.

I was very tempted. I was so very tempted. I blinked as much to break the intense eye contact as to clear my head of everything that was him. "Not going to happen." Even I wasn't convinced by my tone.

He wrapped his arm around me and pulled my body against his. He smelled like a seductive smoke, it was musky and woody with a touch of sweetness like a rich honey. I could feel every muscled ridge, every hardness up against my body. He was taller than me, but he held me so tightly my feet were barely on the floor and my lips weren't that far away from his. Those eyes, pure red now were mesmerising and the ghost of a smirk at his lips made goose bumps break out over my skin. I was hot. It was a good hot, a bad hot, and an amazing hot. My breath was coming a little shallower than I wanted and I knew he'd be able to feel my heart racing in my chest.

"There's no weakness in giving in," he whispered, his lips getting closer to mine.

I was reaching up just as slowly as he was leaning down.

My hand slid up his chest but, before it snaked around his neck, I stopped it and pushed against him. He let me go and I dropped my face for good measure.

"You want to avoid your dad's party? I don't want to go. Tell him we're doing whatever you want, but you could stay here with me?" I raised my eyes and found him looking at me weirdly.

He said nothing. Just looked me over with just as much heat in his still red eyes. Finally, he asked, "And what do you think we're going to do?"

"Talk? Sit in silence? Play chess?"

"I don't do talking."

"Then tell him you're banging me senseless and we'll sit in silence," I huffed.

"I can't lie."

I sighed loudly. "Then, whatever. I'm just trying to help, Drake."

"Why would you even want to talk to me?"

I rolled my eyes. "I don't know. Maybe because I'm stuck here with you and figure I may as well get to know a bit more about you."

He licked his lip slowly and I followed the movement like a desperate weirdo. "I don't have to lie to make my father assume what I want him to. I'll make our excuses."

He grabbed a towel, throwing it around his waist, and headed back into our room.

"Ignacio, go and tell my father we will not be at his party."

"What shall I tell him, boss?" I heard Ignacio growl.

"Tell whatever you need to so he thinks Wren and I are busy. Sexually."

I walked out of the bathroom to see Ignacio nod. He spared a look at me, then was gone. Kyle was sitting in the chair I'd been in and was reading my book. Or at least, the closest approximation I imagined he was capable of, what with the book upside down and all. Truman was hovering as he always did.

"Truman, Wren and I will take dinner in our room alone tonight. You boys may have the night off."

Kyle's face fell as he looked between me and Drake.

"We'll see you tomorrow, sir. Ma'am." Truman bowed and then dragged a protesting Kyle out.

I heard the lock click on our side and knew Drake must have locked it.

We stood, staring at each other for the longest time. My heart thudded in my chest. It was the first time we'd been truly alone since he'd come sauntering back into my life. And he was basically naked. The memory of him being totally naked was still super fresh in my mind. I was having trouble thinking of anything but him being naked just then, and adding myself into the mental mix as well.

"You wanted to talk?" he asked gruffly. "Talk."

I swallowed hard. "So, how *was* your day?" was all I could come up with.

His eyebrow rose, but he answered as he moved to get dressed. "You really want to know?"

I nodded as I curled up in my chair. "I really want to know what you get up to every day."

He gave a huff that almost sounded like a laugh. "It's not pleasant for human ears."

"I can take it."

He threw me a heated look and I rolled my eyes.

"Just tell me."

"All right. Don't say I didn't warn you."

So, while Drake was avoiding spending time with his Dad and I was avoiding the even more stark reminder I was in Hell, we spent the night talking about what was basically his job in Hell. It was just as terrifying and far more interesting than I thought it would be.

Drake

I could have forced her. Of course, I could have. I wanted her six ways from Sunday, that wasn't a problem. The problem was me not wanting to force her.

I'd spent literal ages – like, Ages – watching how well the men in my family forcing themselves on women had gone. Persephone was probably Dad's biggest failure to date. No amount of will he'd tried exerting on her had made her give in to him, even with the might of Demeter behind her to motivate him. And Grandad? I sincerely doubt I needed to go there for any of his manifestations.

So, I was going to do this the old-fashioned – or, the new-fashioned really – way and seduce her properly. I was well-practised in a lot of things sexual, but proper seduction was not one of them. A benefit to being the son of Lucifer was it didn't take a lot of effort on my part to get a woman of any species into bed, in Hell or on Earth. I had a natural power that made any conquest simpler.

Wren was nothing like any woman I'd ever come across. Thus far, getting Wren's interest was proving to create more problems than it was solving. I knew she wanted me as much as I wanted her. It was in her eyes when she looked at me, I could feel it in her heartbeat, and I could literally see into her mind on the two occasions I'd delved in there. But she was still holding on to ridiculous human notions like we had to like each other before we fucked, or Hell-forbid that we fell in love first.

And it was driving me insane.

Until I was going insane for a whole other reason.

I walked in on her changing the day after we didn't go to Dad's party.

When she heard the door, she pulled a blanket up over her body, barely covering anything scandalous. It still left the curve of her waist blossoming into her wide hips on show and that was just as sexy to me as anything else. That and the fact that the forbidden had always been tantalising to me – a curse of my birth.

"What?" she asked and I realised I hadn't said anything for too long.

"A man can't appreciate his wife's body?" I quipped and that's when it happened.

Instead of the chastising look and sigh any sort of flirtation had been met with for the previous week, she bit her lip and chuckled as she turned away.

I was busy marvelling at that fact when I was distracted by the sweet soft skin of her back. Keen to push my luck to the very edge of its boundaries, I walked forward and placed my hands on her waist, dipping my head to breath her in.

"Drake…?" she said slowly. It was a warning and a question.

"Wren?" I replied, running my nose up to her hair.

I could feel her body humming under my touch and I was burning to touch her more. But I could also feel her uncertainty. I didn't need to read her mind to know she wasn't ready. It was in the way she tensed almost imperceptibly. It was in the way she held the blanket against her tighter.

It ate at me to think that was putting me off from going after what I wanted. But what else was I going to do? The men in my family basically invented taking advantage of women because of who we were. Anything I knew would baffle my old man I'd do. And if that meant waiting until Wren was ready, then that's what I was going to do. Every afterlife be damned.

I felt her take a deep breath and relax. She turned to look at me and gave me the smallest smile. It was an apology. I wasn't going to have her apologetic. I wanted her fierce and confidant. I wanted the Wren I knew she was.

"I need to get back," I said softly.

I was trying to respect her boundaries, but I couldn't help pressing a small kiss to her shoulder before I moved away. I left her standing there, refusing to turn back to look at her no matter how much I was tempted for one last glimpse.

"That was quick," Ignacio grunted.

"Shut it," I snapped.

Kyle would have run away from my tone. Truman probably would have said something droll about how well it was going with Wren. But Ignacio was a hellspawn after my own heart. If there was anything he understood, it was anger and annoyance and he relished any opportunity for us to wallow in it. So, he trailed along behind me while I got on with my work.

He came with me to the Torture Grounds, where we looked over the mass torture of the souls drowning in their own guilt and self-doubt. We went to some of the personal hells where I was in a bad enough mood that I took over a couple of times because the demon in charge wasn't skinning the soul quite slowly and agonisingly enough.

"See, Perdix?" I asked the fourth one. "You've got to do it slowly. Then, when they're getting numb to it," I flicked the knife expertly and the soul screamed, "twist and drive it in nice and deep."

Perdix was hovering at my shoulder. "I see, sir. Thank you."

I handed him back the knife and flicked most of the blood off my hands. "Go on, let me see you do it properly."

Perdix nodded and took my place at the soul.

"Thanks so much, Drake," the soul said. "It's so hard to get good help these days."

"Remind me again why you're here?" I asked, rhetorically.

The soul chuckled self-consciously. "Right. Yes. Good point. All I meant was it's a shame it's so busy down here nowadays. Back when your father could do it all him–" He finished on a shriek and I nodded to Perdix.

"Brilliant timing."

"Thank you, sir."

I oversaw Perdix for a few more moments before I headed out to do some more of my rounds, Ignacio still at my heels. We went through the Surrounded in Gambolling Puppies sector, the Watching the Whole Twilight Franchise area, the Firefly Being Cancelled Over and Over division, the Christmas Fruit Pies Being in Stores in October zone, and finally made our way back to a few more of the personal hells.

"Hey, Drake," Rene said when I got to him.

"You've kept to your torment lately. Well done."

"Well, you know." He shrugged. "I said I'd behave. What have we got on the roster today?"

"Let me nibble," Ignacio muttered, licking his lips as he shuffled towards Rene.

Rene laughed nervously. "I mean, sure. We could go with eaten alive. Why not? It's been a while."

I sighed. "It just takes so long. And a guy's got places to be. What do you say we chuck you on the rack for a bit?"

"Maybe over an open flame?"

I nodded. "Nice touch."

We got him settled and I started winding up the rack.

"How is it going with Serenity?" Rene asked between screams.

"Good. I think. I hope. She's starting to warm up to me."

"Oh, hey. That's great. You need any more lines?"

I shook my head. "Nah, thanks, man. You know she smiled at me when I tried one on her today."

"No way?"

I nodded. "Yeah. I wasn't even trying for something that worked. I'm just so horny. You know?"

"I do know. Millenia without sex will do that to a guy."

"I mean, I'm Lucifer's son, for fuck's sake. I'm a prince of Hell, part angel, with the sex drive to match, for Grandad's sake. I just have zero idea how I'm supposed to get her to sleep with me already."

"Aw, sounds like she's special, Drake."

I shrugged. "Yeah, I don't know about that."

"Less romance, more torture," Ignacio growled, his arms crossed.

"Let me talk while I work," I told him. "Helps me concentrate."

Ignacio stabbed me in the foot with a pike. I wasn't going to ask where he got it.

"Ow!" I snapped.

"Pain always helps."

I hated to admit it, but he was right. Pain focused my mind to the task at hand and had the added benefit of motivating me to inflict a lot of pain on someone else.

So, I barely thought about Wren for the rest of my day. When I got back to our room, I found an interesting surprise.

Wren and Kyle were lying in the middle of the floor, their eyes closed. Kyle had a smile on his face. Truman was sitting on a chair, polishing a pair of Oxfords I refused to wear.

"What are you doing?" I asked them.

"I'm carping le diem," Wren said without opening her eyes.

I knew Latin, even bastardised. I was interested to know what she thought it meant, though. "You're what?"

"I'm seizing the day."

"By lying on the floor?"

"Yes."

I shook my head. "I'm not even going to ask," I muttered as I walked to the wardrobe and pulled off my shirt.

"It hums," Kyle sighed happily.

I turned back to look at them and saw Wren smiling at him fondly.

"What hums?" I asked him.

Wren spread her arms out like she was playing at snow angels. "The whole place."

I frowned. "What whole place?"

"Hell."

"Hell hums?"

Wren propped herself up on her elbows and looked at me. "You're the prince of hell. How have you not noticed?"

How the Heaven had she?

I turned away from her to try to calm the force of my heartbeat. It was one thing to be attracted to her body. It was another to find her personality attractive. Because there was something very attractive about the wonder in her voice and her eyes, like, if I let myself, I could get back some of the magic I'd lost through her eyes.

"You should try it sometime," Wren said.

I snuck a look back at her and saw she was lying down with her eyes closed again.

"I get enough of Hell without…lying on the floor."

"Come on. It's amazing. There's this…pulsating rhythm. It's like I can feel it in my soul."

I smirked as I pulled on a clean shirt. "If you want a pulsating rhythm you can feel in your soul, I have just the thing…"

She propped herself up on her elbows again, but she was smiling. "I'll make you a deal–"

"A deal with the devil's son?" I interrupted cheekily. "Naughty."

Her smile grew. "A deal with my husband. You come and feel the pulsating rhythm," I had a lot of naughty thoughts, but her tone of voice intended that, "of your home and I'll consider reconsidering consummating our marriage."

It wasn't the deal that had me tempted to agree, it wasn't what I *might* get out of it, it was about the fact she was open to suggesting such a deal in the first place. As stupid as lying on the floor to feel Hell hum seemed, I was very close to planning on doing it just for her.

"Sir, you might want to remove your trousers as well," Truman said and Wren and I both looked to him for an explanation. Truman looked down and I followed his gaze. "It seems we were a touch enthusiastic with the torture today, sir."

I tried not to look at Wren for her reaction, but I did. And she was looking at me quizzically but not overly judgmentally. "There was a lot of incompetence going around today," I muttered as I pulled my jeans off. Thank Grandad for powers and getting to wear whatever I wanted whenever I wanted.

"And you had to show them…personally?" Truman asked.

I grabbed a pair of trackpants to make Wren more comfortable. "Yes."

"Working off some frustrations, sir?"

"Yes."

"Did it work, sir?"

"No," I hissed. "Isn't there anything else you could be doing now?"

"Feel the hum!" Kyle squeaked, sounding totally blissed out – which was kind of ironic given we were in Hell.

"Thank you. I should clean the blood out of these." Truman picked up my clothes and trotted out with them.

Could he have just incinerated them for fun and then I'd get new ones? Yes. But Truman liked to do things the human way, said it calmed him and made him feel useful in a world full of too much ease. I had to say, as much as I liked calling whatever I wanted into existence, it added a touch of humanity to my day that I yearned for.

"Come on, Drake." Wren patted the floor next to her. "Come and share the pulsating rhythm with me."

My smirk was back. "Pretty daring words, there."

She smirked in response. "Get over here."

I sighed and dragged myself to her, dropping down onto the floor.

"Okay, lie down on your back."

"You like it on top, then?" I joked as I did as she asked.

She nudged me companionably and lay back down next to me. "See?"

"See what?"

"Close your eyes and…feel the hum."

I did close my eyes, but I rolled them heavily first for good measure. I took a deep breath and let myself relax into the floor and…

"I'll be saved," I breathed.

"See?" Wren laughed. "You feel it?"

"It's… Hell hums," I marvelled.

And it did. There was this steady… Wren had put it near perfectly. There was a steady, pulsating rhythm. It was like a heartbeat, but deeper in your bones, your very soul. It felt connecting and, for a place that was literally damned, it felt wholesome. But then that could have been because I was born to the place. Which would explain my connection to it, but…

Wren's hand slid into mine.

I opened my eyes and turned my head to look at her. She was still lying there with her eyes closed and a gentle smile on her face.

If my birth explained my connection to Hell, and it could explain Kyle's, what explained Wren's? And what explained my connection to her?

10
Wren

After making some headway with my relationship with Drake, such as it was, I decided that ten days confined to our room was enough. I woke up and decided that I was going to ask the boys to take me exploring.

Drake was still asleep, so I took a moment to watch him. He looked almost peaceful asleep. All his hate and anger had melted away and left him settled. Although, maybe I was just seeing him differently after the other night. Hearing about what he got up to when he was 'working' had been fairly awful, but it had also given me hope that he could open up to me, and it would make my stay in Hell far more palatable if we at least got along.

I thought I could see a little bit of the old Drake underneath all that darkness. Not that I could really remember him that well. It was more like fragments of who I thought he used to be, reactions to things I thought he should have that he didn't, things he said that sounded wrong and right at the same time.

When Kyle snuffled in his sleep – at my feet at the end of the big bed – I smiled and slipped out as carefully as I could. Ignacio snorted roughly, spreadeagled on my chair.

And Truman was tucked up neatly under a blanket on the couch.

Just as my feet hit the floor, Drake's hand shot out and wrapped around my wrist. My heart thundered in my chest at the suddenness of it and I took a deep breath.

"Where are you going?" he rasped, sounding half-asleep still.

"I was going to shower and get dressed," I said quietly.

Drake blinked. "What time is it?"

It hadn't taken me long to work out that time was a loose construct in Hell, but they still seemed to run on some sort of internal – or, infernal maybe? – clock. I was sort of getting the hang of it.

"Late enough to be getting up. Early enough I was trying not to wake you."

His arm relaxed, but he still held my wrist and he looked blearily up at me. I saw red glowing eyes poking out from beneath his thick lashes. "But everything's okay?" he asked. His voice was rough and husky and I told myself it didn't do anything for me.

"Yes. Why?"

His grip on my wrist slowly relaxed until he was lying back on the bed again. "I just worried," he said with a yawn. "Something felt…portenty."

"Portenty?" I whispered, not wanting to wake the devilbums.

He nodded as he snuggled back against the pillows. "Happens. Portents," he said lazily. "I know something bad's gonna to happen. Always does. You're fine?"

I nodded. "I'm fine, Drake."

"Good. Come back to bed, then," he mumbled, patting the bed next to him absently.

The simple and easy way he said that tugged on my heart. As if it could be that simple. As if we could be like a real couple. As if I wasn't technically-but-not-really just eighteen and in no way ready to be a wife. As if he wasn't the son of the devil and I was a human. Because putting aside everything else, how would that even work long-term?

"I'm getting ahead of myself," I murmured as I slowly slid out of the bed.

But Drake must have gone back to sleep because he didn't stir.

I tip-toed to the bathroom and closed the door, finding myself with the most privacy I'd had in a good few days. Kyle was adorable and Truman was helpful, but a little alone time was just what the demon ordered.

I took my time in the shower, savouring the warm water despite the fact I felt like I'd been living in a sauna.

And I totally hadn't packed appropriately for the weather. I didn't know what I thought Hell was going to be like, but I'd managed to pack all the sorts of things I'd usually be wearing at home in the late Spring. Suffice to say, I was overdressed most of the time and too scared of what I might be given if I asked for anything more suitable.

When I snuck back into the room, Truman was the only other one awake. He was folding his blanket up and nodded to me as I went to the wardrobe.

"Do you need something, ma'am?" Truman asked as I was rifling through the wardrobe for something not so hot.

I bit my lip as I thought about it. This could go all sorts of wrong, but I couldn't keep wearing jeans in Hell.

"If I ask for a dress, what am I going to end up with?"

Truman seemed to think about that for a moment. "What would you like?"

I shrugged. "Nothing fancy, nothing revealing. Just something nice to wear in this heat."

Truman nodded and rubbed his claws together. Suddenly, my towel was in his claws and I was wearing a simple spaghetti strap dress with a flared skirt that went to my knees. I looked down at it, swishing the skirt as a matter of course. It was soft against my skin, nice and breathable.

"Perfect. Thank you."

Truman nodded. "I can arrange for similar items to be available for you if you wish?"

"That would be great, thanks," I replied as I pulled my shoes on.

"Of course, ma'am. Are you studying today? Did you need another book? Or are you still going on yesterday's?"

"Actually…" I started, then looked at Drake as he shouted unintelligibly.

He didn't do anything more than roll onto his back – the sheets down around his waist giving me a lot to perve on – so I assumed he was still asleep.

"Is he…okay?" I asked Truman.

"Eternal torture will scar a man, ma'am. He is as okay as anyone can be down here. Now, you were saying?"

I licked my lip and decided to let it go. That seemed kind of horrible, but Drake's mental state wasn't really my business. "I was thinking you could show me around today?"

"Around…Hell, ma'am?"

I nodded. "Yes. Is that not…allowed?"

"Oh no, ma'am. You have free rein in Hell, as it were. I just wonder about the sense in leaving the…safety of your room?"

I nodded, sub-consciously swishing my skirt again. "I get that. But if I'm going to be here for a while, then I should probably get to know the place. I can't spend eternity in this one room."

"I assure you, ma'am, if you really wanted to, you easily could."

I smiled at him. "Nevertheless, would you mind showing me around?"

Truman breathed out. "No. Of course not, ma'am. I am here to serve. Did you have anywhere particular in mind?"

I shook my head. "I have no idea what there is. Give me the tourist experience."

Truman nodded. "Indeed, ma'am. Would you like to be going now?"

"Just let me leave a note for Drake and then we can get going."

"Capital idea, ma'am."

By the time I was done with my note, Kyle was awake and insisting to come with us. So, the three of us crept out of the room, closing the door behind us quietly.

"Where we going?" Kyle asked, yawning and stretching.

"Miss Serenity wishes to explore," Truman told him. "Would you care lead the way, ma'am? We can act merely as...guides."

I grinned, feeling brighter than I had in days. "All right."

Kyle stuck close to me as we wandered through the halls, and Truman trotted at a more stately pace behind me. The whole place was hot and I felt slick with sweat in no time, but it wasn't unbearable.

"Those are the Torture Grounds, ma'am," Truman explained as I walked up to a lookout.

Underneath us was this huge expanse of space covered in people moaning and stretching upwards as though they were drowning.

"So, they all just… What?" I asked. "What exactly's going on here?"

"They're being tortured by the weight of their guilt, ma'am." Truman came up beside me and boosted Kyle onto his shoulders.

Kyle put his hands on the safety rail and leant forward eagerly as he looked around at all the people below us.

"What did those people do?"

"Souls, ma'am."

"Sorry?"

"They have long since been people. Down here, they're souls. The only real person in Hell at this moment is you."

I nodded. "Right. So, those souls… What did they do?"

"Any number of sins, ma'am. It takes more than one to send you here. Shall we move on?"

Kyle jumped down from Truman's shoulder and started scampering off.

"This way," he called. "Follow Kyle."

"Where are we going?" I asked Truman as we trailed after Kyle.

"I think he wants to show you the good bits, ma'am."

"There are good bits?"

Truman nodded as he kept as eye on Kyle's darting form, but he didn't seem entirely convinced. Kyle barrelled his way through other demons and devilbums and whatever else the other creatures were. Some of them shook pikes and fists at Kyle, some just shook their heads and muttered at him.

"Hell is not a simple place, ma'am," Truman said slowly. "Many of your Earth years ago, there was only one afterlife. His lordship was responsible for all the dead – the good, the bad, the heroic."

"Really?"

Truman folded his arms behind his back as we walked. "Yes, ma'am. Hades was not only his name, but the name of his domain. The rivers flowed free and fast, separating the places in the afterlife. Places that stayed here when the good had another place to go."

"That's…" That was a lot to take in. "Wow."

"Indeed, ma'am. His lordship has had many names and many manifestations in human history. Hell…accommodates, as does his lordship."

"So, Hell is…Hell because of humanity."

Truman nodded. "Indeed, ma'am. Humanity's beliefs mould us."

"Here!" Kyle called. "Here!"

I followed him out of the tunnel and into a brightly lit field. The colours were vibrant – greens, yellows, pinks, oranges, blues. Bunnies bounced around, unicorns frolicked, teddy bears rumbled around happily. There were fruit trees and rainbows and pots of gold. Kyle went running around madly, chasing a few bunnies here and there. It *looked* like paradise to me.

Until a soul went running past me, shrieking in terror. He was followed by a unicorn. Which was all fine until the unicorn caught up to him and knocked him down. A teddy bear then jumped out from behind a bush and started kicking him. Another teddy bear joined in and started smacking the soul with what looked like a rainbow candy stick.

"Oh my God," I breathed, my hand to my chest. "What the Hell?"

"God has absolutely nothing to do with it. Hell, on the other hand…"

"*Why* does this place exist?"

"Some souls have an…interesting definition of Hell. I personally don't see what's so frightening about this field. In the old days, it was all just fire and brimstone and," he thrust his claws forward violently, "good old stabbing."

I smiled. "I see."

"Shall we move on, ma'am?"

I pointed after Kyle – who was head down, bum up and wriggling, as he stalked a teddy bear. "Do we leave him here, or…?"

"Kyle!" Truman said.

Kyle's head popped up among the grass as the teddy bear spotted him and ran off quickly. "Going?"

"We're moving on," Truman said.

I smiled as Kyle ran towards us and then headed off through the field. Souls ran around, being beaten up by unicorns and teddy bears and even flowers. Some just sat and silently screamed as they pointed at a bunny. Others tried stealing money from the cauldrons and got punched in the nose by something popping out of the pile of coins.

We moved through and out of the Rainbow Fields and back into tunnels.

"Larry!" Kyle cried, throwing his arms in the air.

I turned and freaked the Hell out. My hand went to my heart again and I stepped back so far that I ran into the wall behind me. In front of me were four shadowy beings. I'd seen some of their kind at a distance, but never this close. They were like floating robes, no legs or hands at the end of their arms, just frayed shadowy material. Instead of a real head, it was like there were eyes and a mouth in a hood. The mouths reminded me of jack-o-lanterns, jagged as though with pointed teeth. A chill sprinted up my spine just at the sight of them as they leant towards me ominously.

"Hullo, boys," one of them said, and the jagged mouth turned into a smile.

"Larry. Boys. How are you?" Truman asked.

"Oh, you know. Adequately torturous."

Truman nodded. "Good. Have you met Miss Serenity?"

The being that was Larry swooped forwards, looming over me. "I have. How are you Mrs Drake?"

I nodded, vaguely remembering Larry from when I met the devil. "Uh… Good, Larry. Thank you."

"Sing, Larry!" Kyle called, dancing about.

"Oh, I don't know if Mrs Drake wants to hear a song."

There was enough forlorn regret in his voice, I couldn't help but jump to disagree with him. "No. Not at all. I… I'd love to hear a…song."

"Really?"

"It's not necessary, ma'am," Truman said quietly, his hand covering his mouth.

I smiled at Larry. "I'd love to."

Larry seemed to grin as he and the other three beings pulled themselves into a line a little bit away. I'll be honest, I had no idea what to expect from four shadowy creatures in Hell, but it had been ages since I'd heard a song. I was expecting some sort of metal – death, heavy, maybe even Christian. What I got was a barbershop quartet. It was seriously the best part of my trip to Hell so far.

It wasn't a song I recognised, but with a whole human history of music to choose from, that didn't surprise me. By the end of the song, I was smiling warmly.

"That was amazing!" I said, clapping wildly when they were finished.

"Oh. Thanks, Mrs Drake. We needed something to pass the time, you know."

That I didn't doubt.

"We'd love to stay and chat, but we should really go. Turns out some souls consider barbershop a torture," Larry scoffed in humour.

"No?" I asked, realising I found that totally believable but putting on a good show of disbelief for him.

Larry nodded. "I know. Mad. But it gives us something to do. We'll see you later, Mrs Drake."

"Bye, Larry!" Kyle called, waving as the four shadows floated away.

"Well, that was unexpected," I said as we moved on.

"There are…upsides and downsides to different notions of Hell, ma'am."

Everything seemed to be going as well as it could on a tour of Hell. Then Kyle got super excited and Truman got rather anxious. I decided that Truman's lead was probably the one I should follow.

I heard a growl from behind me as though in stereo.

I very slowly turned around.

"Ma'am, don't move!" Truman hissed. "Kyle, get Master Drake. Quickly!"

It didn't matter if I wanted to move or not. I was frozen in utter fear. Big dogs in general were something I was ashamedly uneasy around. Dogs the size of a three-storey buildings with three snarling, drooling heads? Turns out I was no better around them.

Drake

When I woke and found Wren missing, I had a rather embarrassing mini freak out. It woke Ignacio, who launched at me in surprise and attached himself to my face like some sort of startled feline.

"You good?" I asked him.

He nodded and we peeled him off my face. As embarrassed by his lack of decorum as I was by mine, we didn't speak of it.

"The others are gone, she has to be with them," I said as Ignacio snuffled around like he was looking for something.

"Here, boss," he said, holding a piece of paper up to me.

I took it and saw a scribbled note.

"The boys have taken her sightseeing. She'll see us later," I mumbled as I read over the note.

"See?" Ignacio grumbled. "Fine."

I nodded. But it didn't feel fine. I had that weird panicky, indigestion-y feeling that always heralded something going badly for me. Nine times out of ten, the something was hot on the heels of me doing something I knew had consequences. That still didn't put my mind at ease. Especially with Wren wandering around Hell.

I got to work and tried to take my mind off it. But even watching Ignacio eat someone alive didn't have the same distracting effect as usual.

"You seen Cadriel?" I asked a passing demon.

"I think he's in the Training Grounds."

I nodded. "Thanks."

Cadriel was my go-to for stress relief. A little time spent in the pit trying to gouge each other's innards out always made the underworld of difference.

"Morningstar," he said as I strode in. "What can I do for you today?"

"The usual, angel. Arm up."

He threw me a sword and we began circling.

Cadriel was the closest thing I had to a best friend. And that was more because he was the only other being than the devilbums that I spent any significant time with. Even if most of that time was spent trying to kill each other.

But even fighting with Cadriel did little to soothe my unease. Not that he minded me taking it out on him. My sword clashed with his mighty axe, the sound clapping like thunder in the midst of a great and terrible storm.

I was just getting into stride when it was ruined.

"Drake! Drake! Drake!" Kyle huffed as he hurtled into the room, crashing into the rack of weapons. Ignacio had tried to save him, but just ended up further in the weapons rack.

I held a hand up to Cadriel and stalked over to pull Kyle out of the pile. When he was on his feet again, I bent down to his level.

"What's the little guy all in a tizz about now, Morningstar?" Cadriel asked, leaning on his axe-head.

Kyle gabbled far too fast even for me to catch.

"Slow down. What?" I asked the devilbum, the sense of agitation I'd felt all day gnawing again.

Kyle was breathing heavily and his ears were flapping in agitation. I knew who he was worried about at least. I should have worked it out sooner. That impending sense of doom I'd felt all day. I should have known it would have to do with her.

I stood and felt my wings spring out.

"Your wife?" Cadriel asked, his tone telling me what a joke he thought it was, but I didn't have time to answer him.

I just nodded to him. "Where?" I asked Kyle as I threw my sword to Cadriel, who caught it easily with one hand.

"Cerb…" was all Kyle managed to puff but I knew what the rest would have been.

I launched and thanked Grandad that the laws of physics didn't work so well down here as I sailed through the ceiling. I hovered over the bowels and searched. Finally, I saw her. The idiot girl had wandered into Cerberus' personal domain and the great three-headed beast was bearing down on her. If he got his teeth in her, even Grandad couldn't bring her back. Not the way I wanted her.

I dove as fast as my wings would let me, calling to the hulking over-grown mutt in my most authoritative voice. Although, fat lot of good that ever did Dad.

I watched in utter horror as Cerberus beared down on Wren, stalking closer and closer to her. She wasn't moving which, in the circumstance, was the best move. I saw Truman hovering around and knew he would be feeling an awful failure for putting her in danger. I wasn't sure who I was planning on skinning alive first, I was too busy trying to ignore the certain dread I wasn't going to make it to her in time.

I was right.

I was a split-second too late.

Just as I was about to reach her, the unthinkable happened.

I was thrown back into the wall with the force of Cerberus' sudden movement. The powerful torrent of air would have thrown Dad. It would have thrown Grandad. I could only watch, my heart in my throat and my wings fracturing against the wall behind me, as Cerberus threw himself the last distance to Wren and…

And literally threw himself at her feet.

Huxley was centimetres from her toes, Todd and Rocky to either side on his paws. All three of his heads had big goofy doggy grins, tongues lolling on the floor. His butt was in the air and his tail wagged furiously. Wren's dress and hair was blasted backwards as Cerberus breathed out heavily.

"Good dog?" Wren said uncertainly.

Cerberus gave a soft rumbling ruff and dropped his arse on the ground, his tail sweeping the dust into the air around him. Rocky looked at me and barked happily. Wren followed his gaze.

"Drake!" she called. She still wasn't moving and I didn't know whether she was hurt or not after all.

I pulled myself off the wall and ran to her. My arms went around her, my wings instinctively folding around us even as they healed, and she fell into me with a deep breath. Cerberus whined in concern, but there were other things on my mind than pacifying the great big doofus after he scared the living Heaven out of me.

"Are you okay?" I asked, running my hands over her, checking every inch I could see for wounds. My heart beat erratically in my chest and it was not a feeling I enjoyed.

She nodded. "I'm fine. I think."

"Are you sure?"

Something still felt wrong and I didn't know what it was. Panic filled me.

I'd felt this way once in my life. For a whole day, I'd looked over my shoulder. For a whole day, I'd lived with a staccato thudding in my chest and a breath that was never quite caught. And, at the moment I'd almost convinced myself it was nothing, my mother had died – to put a gracious twist on events. Everything in me demanded I remain on high alert, but Wren looked up at me with those big green eyes, shining bright with life and I gave into it. I gave in to her.

As relief flooded through me, I took her face in my hands and I kissed her.

I felt her lean into me for a moment. Her hand on my chest tightened on my shirt. She kissed me back. But just as I was about to bring her closer, she ducked her head and pulled away.

When she looked up at me again, it was with confusion in her eyes. There was no distaste. There was no anger. Just confusion. She blinked and then her eyes shifted behind me and I watched them open in awe. Her mouth dropped open as well and I didn't need to read her mind to know what she was thinking.

"Drake…" she whispered, like she wasn't sure if she could trust her own eyes.

All I could do was nod. There was a reason I'd kept the big reveal hidden. It was because of this. Because of the wonder and pure innocence that flooded her face at the sight of them.

"You've got wings…"

"It doesn't change anything," I told her sternly and I realised I was still shaken after thinking I'd lost her. "What were you doing here?"

She was still looking over my wings. I grabbed her chin and made her look in my eyes.

"Wren. What were you doing here?"

She blinked and seemed to lose a little of the wonder as her focus sharpened. "We were exploring. We went to the Rainbow Field, then Larry sang us a song, then we were here."

"You have to be more careful!" I snapped. "Do you realise how dangerous this place is? How dangerous Cerberus is?"

In great timing on the huge mutt's part, he nuzzled me gently with a soft whine as though it was an apology. I sighed heavily as Wren failed to stifle her smile.

"This one instance aside. I thought I'd lost you!" I finished with a yell, wishing someone would listen to me and my completely founded fears.

All humour fell from Wren's face as she looked me over. "What?"

I took a deep breath and tried to calm down enough to make her listen. "I thought I'd lost you, Wren. Do you understand what that means?"

Naturally, she shook her head. Of course, she didn't know what that meant. Humans never bothered to fully comprehend what their death would mean, why would she have thought about what would happen if she died in Hell?

"You'd be gone, Wren. You would cease to exist in the manner you are now. There are things even my grandfather can't fix. And believe me, he's tried."

"You care."

I blinked. "Excuse me?"

"If I die. You care if I die."

I took her cheeks in my hands and pinned her eyes. "Yes, I care. You scared me half to death just now. And for an immortal being, that's a pretty fair distance."

"Because you'd have to find another wife?" she asked. It was almost a challenge. Like she was daring me to either tell her she was right or…

I couldn't lie. But I didn't have to give her the whole truth. I shook my head. "No."

Her eyes flickered between mine for the space of two very heavy heartbeats where I wasn't sure what her reaction was going to be. I was about to put a stop to my anxiety and say something when she surged forward and kissed me.

My arms instinctively went around her body, holding her close.

This wasn't just two set of lips pressed together, all meaning and no intention. This was all meaning *and* all intention.

Wren's arms wound around my neck, her fingers sliding into my hair and keeping my face close to hers as our kiss deepened.

She tasted just as sweet as she smelled. She was just as soft as she looked. That mask of innocence was just that; a tenuous façade to hide the confident desire below. She was up on tip-toes, her body pressed against mine and held up largely by my arms alone.

My heart kick-started in my chest and I felt the familiar stirring heat of my hard-on for her. My wings were out and I was about ready to fly us straight to our bed, no questions asked. When she caught my bottom lip in her teeth, they bunched along with my back muscles in preparation.

"All right, Drake. I suppose this is a bad time, then?" Larry said from behind me and my wings weren't the only things to go limp.

I pulled away from Wren and leant my forehead to hers. She pressed her lips together and snorted, the playful smile making her eyes even more radiant. Her nose wrinkled as she fought the laugh and I cursed Hell's bad timing.

"Not at all, Larry. What can I do you for?" I asked.

"I was just thinking that we should reinstate Music Mondays."

Wren smirked at my expression of disbelief. I was being distracted from my first real kiss with my wife because Larry wanted to bring back Music Mondays? Why did I have to deal with all this shit?

"Have you mentioned it to my dad?" I asked.

"Oh, yeah. He said it was a great idea. Seemed pretty annoyed he let it lapse for so long. But he has been really into Samba Sundays lately."

There was something for every holy day of the fucking week in this place. I just failed to see what that had to do with me and why it had to matter at that exact moment.

"Then why are you asking me, Larry?"

"Oh, I'm not."

I sighed. "Okay…?" When Larry didn't elaborate, I asked, "Was there a reason you're bringing it up now, Larry?"

"Oh, yeah! His devilness said you got to be in charge. Thought it was about time you had more of the family responsibility. What with you being married now and all."

Leave it to my father to twist the knife in. I knew he wanted me to succeed in the task he'd set. The guy thoroughly enjoyed setting unwanted duties and watching me go through with them whether I wanted to or not. He also liked making it as difficult as possible for me. He probably somehow knew what had just happened and had sent Larry along to interfere. What better way to delay my progress than cock block me in the most depressing way?

"Do you need to go to work?" Wren asked. Her tone was cheeky. She was sassing me.

And I couldn't take her to our room and enjoy it. I had to deal with Hell stuff.

I groaned. "Can you stay safe for like…a few hours and we can pick this up again later?"

Her eyes searched mine like she was trying to burn the memory of this moment in her mind. I completely understood the sentiment; I was busy trying to do the same.

Finally, she nodded. "I can do that."

"Thank Grandad," I muttered.

"I'll see you later."

I nodded, pressed a kiss to her forehead, and turned away from her before I couldn't anymore. "All right, Larry. Talk me through your plan."

12

Wren

All right, so I was over whatever excuse I was telling myself was why I wasn't sleeping with Drake. That was irrelevant. It was stupid. It was all lies anyway.

There were only good repercussions for sleeping with him.

I lost nothing.

Nothing except him.

In one swift move, the very best outcome from sleeping with him had suddenly become far less enticing.

Of course, I wanted to go home. I missed my family. I missed Harmony. Did it help that I knew for a fact they'd probably only experienced a few hours of my absence and Drake had made them all totally okay with me being gone? Of course, it did. But I'd still experienced almost two weeks without people I loved and saw every day, and I was missing them.

But going home also meant the very real possibility that I'd never see Drake again. And even if I did, so much time might have passed for him that he wouldn't look at me the same way anymore, he might not touch me the same way. And there was something very unattractive about that prospect.

Suddenly, my not sleeping with him had nothing to do with some imaginary principles and everything to do with me being afraid he'd send me home after I did. Even if Drake didn't send me home right away, his father might.

Not that it was the most pressing matter just then.

When I heard the bedroom door open, I spun around quickly only to find it was one of those rolly-polly guard demons with the pike, the helmet, cropped leather vest and black diaper – for all intents and purposes.

"His devilness, Lucifer, Lord of all Hell and your beguiling father-in-law would like to invite you to dine with him and the family tonight, ma'am," it intoned and I fully believed it was a direct message from said father-in-law.

"Uh…" I started, thinking it was Neville, but not sure. "Thank you…Neville…?"

A smile of cracked teeth erupted on his face. "You're welcome, ma'am. Master Drake is already there, if you're ready?"

"Oh." I looked around the room. Kyle grinned at me, Truman waited for instruction, and even Ignacio seemed waiting for my word. "Oh. Um. Yes. Sure."

I took a step forward.

"His devilness was quite clear on the dress code, ma'am," Neville said apologetically.

"What does he want?" Truman asked, sounding exasperated.

"He wants it to be quite formal."

"Of course, he does," Truman sighed. "All right, ma'am. Let's get you dressed."

If Hell had its own version of a Cinderella-moment, this was it. Only instead of a fairy godmother, I had a Truman. Instead of mice, I had an ignacio. Instead of a pumpkin, I had a Kyle. And instead of the wonderous magical transformation, mine involved more fire and less coverage.

I was left standing in a tight black dress. Half the bodice was nothing but beading, exposing an unnecessary amount of skin. On the same side, there was a slit up the skirt that went almost to my hip and met the sheer half of the bodice, but at least it meant I could walk while I was flashing my entire leg to the whole of Hell. It was paired with some tall, black mary-jane heels. I could feel my hair was up, with annoying wispy bits tickling my neck and cheeks.

"Truman…this is… I can't wear this."

"On the contrary, ma'am. You are wearing it."

"No, I meant–"

"If you're ready, ma'am," Neville said from the door.

I sighed. "Fine. Fine. Who needs modesty anyway?"

I tucked some of my skirt in my hand to make walking even easier and followed Neville to my father-in-law's throne room.

At the doors, I took one more look down and I tucked some hair behind my ear. As I looked up again, I found the doors were open and everyone inside was staring at me.

"There you are, Serenity!" my father-in-law called.

"Inside!" Kyle whispered from behind me, giving me a gentle nudge.

I stumbled forward, and tried to make it look like normal forward momentum.

At least I wasn't the only one dressed up to the ninth circle of Hell.

Esther had swapped her swathe of sheer fabric for a severe white gown. The off-the-shoulder design swept out from her body in points. It cut into her waist like her waist barely existed. The train was quite long but, since she seemed to sort of hover and float ominously rather than walk, it didn't seem to be a problem.

"You look wonderful, daughter," my father-in-law said with a wicked gleam to his eye.

He wore a red tuxedo, complete with tails. His hair was slicked back, horns shining proudly. His cane had a silver skull at the top. His Oxfords were white and black and polished to perfection.

"Thank you…your lordship."

He scoffed with a grin. "No. No. That won't do at all." He stood up from his throne and swaggered towards me, swinging his cane. "No wife of my son will endure such…formalities." He pointed to Drake then to me. "Doesn't you wife look *fetching*, son?"

I'd avoided looking too closely at Drake because I needed the brain power for walking in those shoes. But I had no choice then and I did almost roll my ankle.

Drake was in a similar tuxedo to his father. But where the devil's was red, Drake's was white. It contrasted against his near-black hair and olive skin brilliantly. It even made his blue eyes shine. Not that they stayed blue for long. Our eyes locked across the basically empty room and I watched as they went bright red, glowing brighter than his father's ever had. He was walking towards me as though under his father's sway.

"Doesn't she look…good enough to…eat," the devil purred, then his manner changed from seductive to chirpy. "A woman like that – the wife of my only living son – surely she's earned more familiarity than 'your lordship'. No, no, Serenity. You will call me Lucifer. Satan if you wish. Hades if that's your preference. Or even…Daddy, if you're feeling naughty." He winked at me. "But never 'your lordship'."

By the end of his speech, Drake was standing in front of me and music had started.

"Now." Lucifer threw his arms up and we were surrounded by hundreds of couples. "We dance!"

Drake's eyes burned in more ways than one as he looked down at me. The memory of our kiss seared me just as deep as he picked my hand up gently and lay it on his shoulder. As he took hold of my other hand, it went to my waist – the one barely covered in beading – and my skin blazed pleasantly at his touch.

Lucifer was singing a song I didn't recognise. It was slow and rough, the vocals deep and the tune almost jagged. But every couple – even Drake and I – danced the same steps as they twisted and twirled around the room in perfect sync. I didn't know if it was kudos to Drake's leading skills or some magic in the music. I suspected the latter.

But at least I didn't have to think about the steps as I stared at my husband – when the dance permitted. My mind was completely free to fantasise about him, to lust over him, and to imagine we hadn't been interrupted earlier.

The whole scene had something mystical and magical about it that left me in a foggy state of lust. I could think of nothing but Drake's hands on my body and his lips on mine as he ripped me out of my dress.

I lost track of the number of dances. I only knew that, at some point, Drake, Lucifer, Esther and I were sitting at the table – occupying the same seats as my first night in Hell. The other couples still danced like puppets on strings, eerie and silent but for the swishing of skirts. I still couldn't take my eyes off Drake as the food arrived and Lucifer prattled about something he seemed to find exciting.

"Oh, for the Almighty Drip's sake," Lucifer eventually cried, flinging his arms up. "The sexual tension between the two of you is putting me – me of all beings – off my food. Will you go and relieve yourselves and put us all out of your misery?"

I watched Drake look at his father. Lucifer nodded once and flicked his hand towards the door.

"Go. Take her. I have no interest in this puppy love nonsense."

Drake pushed himself up from the table with enough force the chair went flying backwards, dancing couples manoeuvring seamlessly to let it clatter past. But I was too tense to find anything funny about the situation, even with Lucifer's little exclamation of surprise.

Drake stalked around the table and held his hand out to me. I put my hand in his more than willingly.

"Yes. Yes. Very intense. Very romantic." Lucifer waved his hand at us to hurry up.

Drake pulled me up and didn't stop pulling as we practically jogged back to our room. Until we reached the door. He drew me to him with one arm and kissed me as he threw the door open with his other hand. Lifting me over the threshold and closing the door behind us, his lips didn't leave mine.

Then I was falling forwards as he fell backwards and he wrapped me up tight against him as his back hit the floor.

"Hello!" Kyle said, his head popping up next to Drake's shoulder, a smile stretching ear-to-ear. "We fell."

Drake cleared his throat as he tried to sit up and I scrambled to be more helpful in that endeavour. "Hi, Kyle."

"Good dinner?" Kyle's ear twitched.

I nodded to Kyle, not wanting to be rude but also really needing to get back to kissing Drake. "It was nice, yes."

"I see we can't even make it to the bed now, sir," Truman said smoothly.

"Barely got in the door," came Ignacio's growl and I looked at him to see what passed for a smile on his face.

"Do you think you boys could give us the room?" Drake asked pointedly.

"Why?" Kyle asked, his head cocking to one side, then the other as he took us in.

"Why do you think?" Ignacio huffed the roughest laugh in the history of rough laughs.

"Indeed. How long do you need, sir?" Truman asked.

"Give us the night," Drake said.

"As you wish. Good night, sir. Ma'am."

"Good night," I said as he and Ignacio started moving out.

"Kyle stay. Kyle help!" he said joyfully, bouncing on his hooves.

"Nope," Ignacio darted back into the room to pull him out.

The devilbums closed the door behind them and I heard the tell-tale sound of the door locking.

"Where were we?" Drake's deep voice brought me back to the right moment.

As I turned back to him, he took my hand and pulled me into his lap and kissed me hard. It was possessive. It was demanding. It was passionate. It was everything you wanted in a kiss. Most importantly, it was needy.

Drake kissed me like there was only me. I had never felt so wanted. I hadn't known it was possible to feel that wanted. I felt it in the depths of who I was. It started in the centre of my soul and spread through my body, coursing along my veins, skittering along my skin. It spread until I felt a whole new sense of heat. One that came with a sense of peace. Something missing had been found. Something wrong had been put right.

I was in Hell. I was all-but married. But nothing in my life had felt more normal.

Which is why I couldn't sleep with Drake.

I pulled away from him, breathing so hard I felt like I'd run a marathon. Drake was far more composed, with just a slightly faster rise and fall of his chest. It was the red of his eyes that gave him away.

"We… I can't," I panted.

I'd expected resistance. I'd expected some sort of bargaining. I'd expected persuasion.

But he nodded. "Okay." The only sign he was as affected as me was a slight breathlessness to his voice.

"Okay?" I wasn't sure if I was pleased or annoyed he'd accepted it.

He nodded again as he ran his hands over my hair softly. "Okay. Slow."

Slow. I didn't want slow. But I also wasn't ready to leave him.

He helped me stand, then we undressed leisurely. He kissed me now and then. It was still full of heat, but less urgency and, as much as I already missed it, I knew it was for the best.

We climbed into bed and he seemed perfectly happy just to kiss me. By the time a normal fire would be little more than smouldering ash, we'd fallen asleep. But, when I woke in the morning, I was tucked into his body and his arm was over my waist.

13
Drake

I wasn't sure how it had happened, but it felt like Wren and I were in some sort of unspoken agreement. She'd been in no hurry to take our relationship any further. Not that we'd had much opportunity, but it felt almost like anything *but* sex was fair game.

I wasn't complaining.

Much.

My father had assured her that she would go home after we slept together. It was a promise not easily broken, and one my father would be keen to keep despite what I may have wanted. Collection didn't equal trophy in our world. I was owed a wife, not a soul. The fact that she was owed my soul in the marriage pact was irrelevant. Her soul did not belong to Hell, ergo she'd go back.

My father had strict rules when it came to souls being where they belonged. If he wasn't strict about it, he could hardly complain when the other team bent the rules.

Which was why he was in such a contradiction when it came to the predicament he had solidly landed me in.

For all his numerous sins, I had to hand it to him. I was pretty sure that, as much as he seemed happy to cock block me on as many occasions as possible. He also seemed to be going out of his way to stir the romance between me and Wren. Romance that was yet to evolve into sex. Only partly due to him. And he was getting impatient.

"I just don't understand why you haven't done the deed yet, son," my father said, hanging over the arm rests of his throne. "You're good-looking. She's good-looking. The two of you are a match made in Hell." He grinned at me proudly. "Literally."

I crossed my arms. "How's Persephone lately?"

Dad waved a hand. "As beautiful as ever. Of course."

"She should be back by now, surely?"

"She has never once in eternity been late. Stop trying to goad me into forgetting what I'm talking about." He sat up and pointed at me. "Is it really that hard to fuck your wife, son?"

"I could ask you the same thing."

Dad gasped. "You wouldn't dare!"

"Wouldn't I?"

"What a husband and wife get up to is their own business!" he said petulantly.

I nodded. "Exactly."

He waggled his finger at me. "No. No. See it's different. A parent gets to meddle. A child doesn't."

I rubbed my nose. "What was Grandad's number again?" I asked, feigning nonchalance.

Dad crossed his arms and slunk down in his throne. "Jumped up, arrogant sod."

"I'll bet he'll be totally thrilled about me seducing a human woman. Third generation for the win!" I said sarcastically.

"Oh yes," Dad mocked. "He'd be so proud. Walking around all righteous and holier than thou up there." He pointed at me. "Back in the day, I knew who he was." He scoffed. "He thinks he's all clever, hiding his past from everyone? Hello? All that smiting. Lightning anyone? You're not fooling anyone, old man," he finished with a mutter, his arms crossed again and a pout like a child sent to the naughty step.

Which wasn't too far from the truth, really. In almost every manifestation of my father, he'd been sent to Hell by Grandad as punishment for disobedience. It just ran in our veins and I was no exception.

"You finished with your daddy issues?" I asked.

"Says you." Dad huffed. "But yes." He waved his hand for me to continue. "Give me your excuses then."

"I'll sleep with her when I sleep with her," I told him.

"How very enlightening." He rolled his eyes, then they narrowed on me and he sat forward. "Say that again."

I frowned. "What?"

"Say that again. Tell me again your excuse."

I shook my head but knew it was better to placate him. "I'll sleep with Wren when I sleep with her."

"Woooo!" he cooed, batting his eyes and clasping his hands under his chin. "Methinks someone's falling for the little human."

"You can think whatever you like, old man," I huffed.

Dad got that look in his eyes. The maliciously mischievous one. The one where he was sure something was going to happen and it was going to be gloriously awful for the soul involved. And he was looking forward to watching it all unfold in the front row with a bucket of popcorn.

"Tell you what. If you're not in love with her when she finally gives into you, I'll ride naked through the streets of Coventry–"

"No one enjoys when you go Godiva, Dad."

He huffed sullenly. "Fine. But don't say I didn't offer."

I gagged a little just remembering the last time he'd decided to Godiva around Hell. "No one would accuse you of that."

He grinned as he spun to lounge on his throne armrests again. "I am a very generous gentleman."

"That's one word for it."

"If you're going to be no fun, you can go about your business."

"Oh, thanks," I replied sarcastically.

"What do you have going on today? Is it beating the ever-fallen nightlights out of Cadriel? Impaling him in place of your wife, perhaps?"

He snuck a look at me, but I wasn't going to rise to the bait. Sometimes I did, as much for entertainment as out of a serious lack of impulse control. But I wasn't in the mood for trading insults with my old man.

"No? Fine," he said sullenly. "A date with the VIPs, perhaps?" He clapped his hands. "Planning our next Music Monday?"

I shook my head. "Larry's learning the meaning of delegation. He's doing a very good job."

"If I don't hear some Gilbert and Sullivan, there will be Heaven to pay. Everyone likes a good barbershop–"

"No, they don't."

Dad rolled his eyes. "Ugh. You're bringing down my vibe, son. Don't tell me what you're doing. See if I care. Just go and do it. I'll sit here by myself and twiddle my thumbs."

"You'll survive, I'm sure."

Dad huffed and dismissed me with a wave. "Be gone."

I gave him a sardonic bow and swept out.

Truth be told, I had a lot of things to do. Souls weren't in the habit of torturing themselves, even after all those centuries endured. But the only thing I cared about on my to-do list was Wren. Not that I was planning on ticking that off any time soon if I could help it.

When I walked into our room, I wasn't sure how much longer I'd be able to abstain.

"Oh, hey," she said with a warm smile as she looked up from her book.

"Reading again?"

She nodded. "This one is at least for school."

"You planning on having them memorised rote before…"

I did *not* want to finish that sentence. I didn't want to think about when she inevitably had to leave. Whether we consummated our marriage to Dad's approval or not, she'd have to go home at some point.

Before I could shake myself out of my unpleasant thoughts, she was standing in front of me and sliding her arms around my neck slowly. Her fingers played with a lock of hair at the nape of my neck and it was a weirdly calming feeling.

"Let me take your mind off it," she whispered as she reached up to kiss me, like she could read my mind and anticipate my needs.

It was at once a reminder of and a solace against her inevitable departure. My mind warred with my heart – one panicking and one feeling far too at ease in her presence – but my body won out and I lifted her up and pushed her against the bed post. Her legs went around my middle like it was instinct.

We lined up perfectly. Like we were made for each other.

It was a torment and a gratification, but I had no plans to change anything.

Her arms tightened around my shoulders as my lips trailed down her cheek to her neck. I felt her sigh in pleasure, her breath tickling my ear. She released me with one hand, reaching up to hold onto the bed post above her head. The arm around me tensed along with her knees around my waist.

I pressed into her, knowing this wasn't going all the way but unable to help myself. Wren moaned against me and I claimed her mouth with mine again.

She kissed me hungrily, like a woman possessed.

I knew how she felt. I felt the same. She occupied my every waking thought. I dreamt about her. I had never wanted anything more in my existence than I wanted to sink myself into her and bring her to the pinnacle of ecstasy, time and time again until the end days. But the overriding need to keep her gave me an unfamiliar level of control over my impulses.

My whole body felt alive to her and only her, but I was in no hurry to satisfy my own desires. I was, though, very interested in satisfying hers.

I slid my hand up her leg slowly, up under her dress. She'd taken to wearing them a lot more lately and I wanted to take full advantage of it. I brought my lips back to her neck and my hand slid between us. The angle wasn't perfect, but I could take her weight with one arm for the sake of her satisfaction.

As I slipped my fingers between her legs, she shivered and another happy sigh tickled my hair. More deliberate this time, I stroked her. Her back arched off the post and into me. I looked at her with cocky pride. Her eyes were closed, there was a soft smile on her face and she was gripping the post above her head firmly.

Slowly, her eyes opened. She looked right into mine as she bit her lip cheekily. Those green depths were full of mischief, desire, heady need. She wasn't just happy for me to continue, she wanted it. But, in a very un-Morningstar move, I checked. Keeping slightly to normal behaviours, I did it in my own way.

"You want me to please you?" It wasn't really a question.

She nodded.

"Tell me what you want," I commanded.

Her chest rose as she breathed in. "I want you to please me, Drake."

My restraint was almost at breaking point. Some of it would be sated by giving her exactly what she wanted, though. So, I didn't hesitate.

I kissed her again as I slid my hand into her panties. She twitched adorably as my fingers touched her bare. She chuckled self-consciously against my lips and I deepened our kiss.

My fingers stroked her gently, always desperate to touch more but not wanting to rush her pleasure. I teased her clit softly, flicking my finger against her and she shuddered as she bit her lip again. Her lips seemed far too distracted for kissing, so I lazily took mine down to her neck again as I worked her.

Wren's body tightened and relaxed at different intervals and I took great pleasure in trying out different methods to see what her reaction would be.

When I slid a finger into her, she gasped then sighed. Her sigh died into a moan as I pumped her. My hips rocked involuntarily with my rhythm; my cock desperate to be the one inside her. But a finger would have to do.

And do it did.

I felt her tighten on my finger and she cried out wordlessly. Her cry became a husky chuckle and she breathed heavily. I slowly slipped my finger out of her, rubbing her softly as the aftershocks made her twitch. I watched her, completely entranced with the soft joy on her face. Her cheeks were flushed and, when she opened her eyes, they sparkled brightly.

"I'm guessing a comment about taking me to Heaven would go down poorly now?" she asked cheekily.

I couldn't help but smirk. "It wouldn't be totally inappropriate. But I can think of something that would go down better."

Her eyebrow rose, but I don't think she was thinking the same thing I was. "Oh? What?"

I felt my most devilish grin growing.

"Drake?" she asked slowly.

Lifting her a little more, I turned and threw her onto the bed. Wren yelped and laughed.

"What are you doing?"

"Showing you what will go down perfectly."

Her mouth dropped open into a little 'o' for a moment, then she smiled and her legs parted slightly. "I do prefer hands-on learning."

Damned Heaven, she was going to be the death of me. Me, an immortal being. And I was going to love every second of it.

14

Wren

I was getting out and seeing more of Hell.

It was either that or risk losing my semblance of control with Drake and probably never see him again. So, sightseeing it was.

Which had me sitting next to my father-in-law under a tattered canopy in a closed off section of an amphitheatre. The rest of the stands were filled with demons and devilbums and souls and whatever sort of creatures Larry and his barbershop quartet were. Esther was nowhere to be seen and, for the moment, neither was Drake. Kyle sat at my feet, Ignacio sulked in the corner, and Truman stood next to me in case I wanted anything.

"Well, then!" the devil cried, his voice carrying around the amphitheatre. "Are we ready to have a little fun on Tussle Tuesday?" He spared me a grin and an eyebrow waggle, then lifted his hands and spotlights and coloured lights started streaming around the place. "It's the showdown of the week! Your favourite pairing! Every time they meet, you get a different ending. Welcome to the stage, our resident Nephilim and his glorified babysitter, the angel who puts the gory into Grigori!" He looked at me again, seeming very pleased with himself. "It's Drake versus Cadriel!"

There was a blast like confetti canons had gone off everywhere and all the light streamed upwards to show two winged figures soaring down into the amphitheatre.

Drake's pure white wings shone with their own luminescence. His torso glistened in the lights, naked but for two crossed straps of leather. He wore black pants and his feet were bare. In his hand, he held a sword that would have been as big as at least two of the devilbums.

Cadriel's wings were black, but were in their own way as beautiful as Drake's. He was clothed in the same fashion as Drake, but wielded a giant axe that was as tall as him. He wore a scowl to give my husband a run for his money as he looked around the theatre.

As they alighted to the floor, they were obviously speaking, but their words didn't reach me.

"Are we ready?" the devil hollered, waving his arms around. "Carnage! Bloodshed! Extra torture if you catch a limb!"

The crowd whooped and cheered, but my eyes were on the two winged men. Cadriel shook his head and Drake almost smiled. Something else was said, then they bumped the backs of their fists together.

"Let's see if we can't scare the little human." The devil looked at me cheekily then dropped his hand and a great clang like a gong sounded and the fight began.

It was like one of those epic battle scenes in a movie. Drake and Cadriel swung their weapons one-handed, like they weighed nothing, when I was sure I'd be hard pressed to even lift them with all my strength. Every hit clashed like thunder through the amphitheatre. When their bodies hit the floor, dust burst around them and, when they got up, there was a definite indent where they'd landed.

The walls of the amphitheatre cracked under their force. Souls and hellspawn went flying if they didn't scurry out of the way and got caught in the crosshairs. The crowd didn't seem to be on either Drake's or Cadriel's side, they were all on the side of violence. And they got violence.

I felt a thrill run through me when the first blood was spilled. I felt sick in my stomach, not just because my head told me Drake was in danger but also at the pure spectacle on display. That wasn't all though, there was something else as well. Some other feeling that wasn't disgust.

It wasn't concern.

It wasn't fear.

It was excitement.

I was enjoying it.

A not insignificant – and growing – part of me was enjoying the show. I was invested. Would Drake avoid that swing of Cadriel's blade? Would his sword connect on the next sweep? My adrenalin was spiking. My heart was in my throat. My butt was at the edge of the seat, my fingers gripping the side of it until my knuckles were white. I couldn't look away if I wanted to. I had to know every move that happened.

Watching Drake's raw power was incredible. On some level, I appreciated it in a purely objective way. It was impressive. There was no question about it. His body moved in a smooth, controlled way whether he was attacking or defending. It was like the two of them were engaged in a deadly dance, sometimes on ground and sometimes in the air.

But I'd be remiss not to admit that a larger portion of me was just one giant lust ball. There was something intensely sexy about watching him fight. About knowing how much precise control he had over every muscle and how deliberate and powerful he was with every movement.

Every fist Drake connected with Cadriel got me excited. Every drop of blood that splattered onto the sandy floor made me want him to whisk me away to our room. It was animal. It was primal. It spoke to me on some deep, primordial level. And I wasn't ashamed to admit it. Not in Hell.

And I realised I liked that. I liked that I could think, feel, act however I wanted and not feel censored or judged. Because, let's face it, the odds were that almost every soul in there had thought, felt or acted worse in their life and probably their death too.

I heard a low chuckle to my left and my eyes slid to the devil.

"Hell looks good on you, daughter," he said proudly.

"You approve of your son's human wife?" I asked him, feeling emboldened by my newfound realisation.

He grinned at me. "He could have chosen far worse."

"I'll take that as a compliment."

"As well you should."

There was an audible sigh of disappointment in the crowd and I looked to the fighters. Cadriel had lost his axe, one wing was bent at a bad-looking angle, and Drake's sword was at his throat.

Lucifer stood up, throwing his arms into the air and smiling widely.

"We have a winner! That was a quick one. Disappointing. Excellent show everyone. Let's get cleaned up and ready for the next one."

I was in the middle of looking for the best route down to Drake when his wings expanded again and he soared up to me. His eyes were red and he breathed heavily.

"We're going," was all he said before he wrapped an arm around me and took off again.

I pressed my face into his chest as my stomach seemed to drop out of my arse. Everything seemed to right itself, so I snuck a peek around and slammed my face back again.

We were I didn't even know how many hundreds of thousands of miles above the bowels of Hell. Just hovering like it was nothing. I'd never been good with heights, and that had been when I wasn't dangling above literal fire and death.

But I'd found no fear in Hell. And I wasn't going to let it stop me again.

I took a deep breath and pulled my face out of Drake's chest to look around again.

It was like Autumn. Reds. Oranges. Yellows. Browns.

Sure, it was fire and blood and torment and never-ending tunnels, but there was actually a weird beauty in it. I could almost see the Rainbow Fields, as a patch of vibrancy in the similarity of the rest of Hell. There were other similar pockets that broke up the monotony. But as not awful as it was, I could only deal with being that high up for so long.

"Were we going to stay here forever?" I chuckled awkwardly.

Drake huffed a rough laugh, held me tighter and said, "You might want to close your eyes again."

I wasn't going to snub that advice. No sooner than my eyes were closed did Drake start diving. I wasn't sure if I was screaming or not. If I was, the sound was being left behind.

I finally felt the world still again and my feet hit the ground. I took a shaky breath to try to calm the furious rampage of my heartbeat and tried to peel myself off Drake.

The lingering feeling of terror was suddenly replaced with a feeling of dread, deep down in my stomach. I turned slowly and saw a spectre floating towards us. It was like Larry, only more corporeal and, instead of a shapeless head, there was definitely a hood. Where the face should have been was just…black nothingness, like a black hole in eternity. The robes didn't fray into nothing, but there still weren't any hands visible and the material dragged along the ground. If I wasn't in the middle of a mild panic attack, I would have joked the robe was too big for whatever that was.

"Hey, what's up?" Drake said to it.

It stopped close to us then moved forward as though it was stepping.

"Wren, this is Death," Drake said.

The hood bobbed like a nod. "Thane is fine. Really."

What was going on?

"Thane?" I clarified, my voice a mere squeak.

"Well, Thanatos. But that's so clunky these days, you know." He leant towards me. "Don't want the hipsters thinking I'm one of them. Just easier to go by Thane."

I nodded, still confused. "I think the robe and the hood might be a dead giveaway on that one." Too late I realised my word choice.

Not that Thane seemed to mind. "Haha. Nice one." He threw his hood back and he was smiling like he thought it was a great joke.

And Death did not look like I'd expected.

I'd grown up with the whole skeleton idea. Fearsome, the skeleton a constant reminder of our own mortality. The robe and the pallor of his features were about all that looked familiar.

Death flicked back his roguish black hair as he smiled. His eyes were almost normal, except his irises were black like it was one big pupil. Or maybe it was. He had a timeless quality to him. His eyes seemed to hold all the wear of a long lifetime, but his starkly chiselled, almost gaunt face was unlined. Had he been human, I wouldn't have been able to guess his age. He wasn't unattractive, but there was a wholly inhuman quality to him that made me a little bit wary around him.

All dread had left me, though. The sense of impending doom had lifted. I felt…as normal as ever.

"What are you guys up to now?" Thane asked, raking a hand through his hair.

Drake looked at me almost in question.

"I think a long, hot shower is in order," I answered.

Thane frowned in confusion. "Shower's aren't necessa… Oh!" he chuckled, tapping the side of his nose. "Oh. I get you. Well, I won't keep you. Souls to reap and all that."

Drake put his arm around my shoulder. "See ya, Thane."

"Reap you later, dude." Thane flipped his hood back up and shook his hand out. A great big scythe appeared in his hand. "Lethal meeting you, Wren." He tapped the scythe's handle on the floor and then was gone in the blink of an eye.

I really shouldn't have been as shocked by that encounter as I was. "That was Death. The Death. The guy responsible for collecting all the dead?"

Drake inclined his head as we continued – walking this time – back to our room. "Well… Soul collection is a tricky process. Thane's job is to ensure all souls cross to the afterlife, making sure none get stuck in limbo – thank Dante for that one. There's an angel of death…"

"I take it we don't like him." I could tell by the way Drake had said it.

Drake's chuckle was humourless, but he smiled. "We don't."

"So, what does this guy we don't like do?"

"Samael's job is judgement. Basically, he's got himself a whole system set up to judge people's lives. You fail, you don't get into Heaven. Not that it's a competition. Hell wants souls. Heaven likes to think they're an exclusive club that few are good enough to enter."

"What does your grandfather do?"

"Grandad?" Drake scoffed. "Watch, mainly. He likes to let the angels do their thing. Samael puts on a good show, but a lot more souls get in than he'd like."

"Because they deserve it?"

He nodded as he opened the door for me. "It doesn't take much to get into Heaven, to be judged a decent human."

"Can you choose to go to Hell?"

"Why?" he asked, suspicion written all over his face.

Certainly not because I'd been wondering about it. "No reason. But even if you were a decent human, can you choose to go to Hell?"

"I'm not sure why anyone would want to."

"Would you choose to go to Heaven? If you could?"

He scoffed again. "With those pompous raging arseholes?" He looked at me and took a breath like he was steeling himself. "Heaven wants me dead. For real dead, not the kind where I wake up in an afterlife and dick about for eternity." He lay a hand on my cheek. "It's impossible for me to put aside a millennium of history between them and me to even begin to find you a real answer to that question."

I put my hand over his. "That sounds like it sucks."

He huffed a laugh. "Yeah. That's one way of putting it."

I stepped away and started pulling my dress off. Drake's eyes were pinned to mine, a red glow starting in those blue depths. I dropped the dress behind me as I started for the bathroom.

"Going somewhere?" he asked.

I nodded, trailing my hand along the door frame. "I *really* feel like a shower…" I smirked at him before I slid out of view.

Drake was in the room with me before I'd taken another two steps. He wrapped his arms around my stomach and held me close.

"You know how to test a man's limit, Serenity…" he whispered.

"And what about a Nephilim? Are his limits higher or lower?"

"There is nothing angelic about what I'm thinking right now."

I turned in his arms and looked into bright red eyes. "How much of you is demonic?"

He stepped forward, forcing me to step back until my back hit the wall of the shower. "How much demon can you handle?"

I looked him over. "Oh. I'd say at least six feet."

His eyebrow rose and his lips tipped into a cocky half-smile. "That's a lot of demon."

"You saying you're not demon enough?"

"Baby, you bring out the demon in me."

He picked me up and pressed me against the wall, nestling between my legs like he belonged there. He was still covered in blood and dirt, but it just added to his natural scent and made me heady with desire for him.

Suddenly, the water cascaded around us and Drake pulled back in surprise. I got my feet under me just in time to not fall on my face half-naked in the shower.

"Thought you could do with a hand, boss," Ignacio grunted.

Drake shook his head, water still streaming down over him. He looked at the devilbum in a combination of gratitude and disbelief. He was breathing heavily, the water being blown by his every exhalation. I wasn't sure if I was waiting for him to rip Ignacio a new one or thank him.

After what felt like an age, Drake shook himself out again and lifted his face to the water. Another couple of heartbeats passed and Drake looked at Ignacio again. He gave the devilbum a single nod. Ignacio nodded back and left, closing the door behind him.

"Do I want to know that was?" I asked.

"Ignacio had a feeling I need to…cool off."

I ran my hand up his chest. He grabbed my hand and held it still.

"Serenity, you keep touching me and I might have to touch you back."

I didn't know if there was an unspoken agreement between us that we were both putting off consummating our marriage as long as possible, or if it was just something I'd made up in my head. But there were other ways to reach mutual relief without Biblical consummation. It was time I did a little tempting of my own.

"Then touch me," I dared him.

"Wren..."

His eyes flashed. I could tell he was torn. I could only hope it was because he also didn't want this to end soon. Everything else told me he wanted this as much as me, so that was the only conclusion I could come to.

I leant up to his ear. "There's still *a lot* of things we can do..." I whispered, taking a chance and hoping it panned out.

He took a single heartbeat to react.

As he kissed me, he hooked his fingers in my undies and pulled me to him. My body crashed into his, but there was no bounce as he held me hard against him. My hand slid down and over his erection.

He paused, his lips not moving against mine. There was a slow rumbling growl in his chest I could feel more than hear. His whole body was tense as though he was trying to control himself.

Before I could say or do anything, he spun me around and pressed me into the tiled wall. It was the only cool thing I'd experienced in the last three weeks. His erection pressed into the base of my back, hard but hot. As he kissed my neck, his hand slid between my legs and he rubbed me with just the right amount of pressure to tease but also send tiny, zinging shockwaves through my body.

I wanted to turn around, to wrap my arms around him, to kiss him, to take him inside me and finally ease the ache just the thought of him created. But it was like he knew my intentions. His body behind mine was immovable, comforting and dominating.

"Behave," came the low growl in my ear.

"You afraid you'll lose control?" I teased, slightly breathless from the sensation he was eliciting between my legs.

"I'm surprised I haven't yet," he said, his fingers dragging tantalisingly over my clit.

I sucked in a breath of pleasant surprise. He didn't want me talking and his hand was ensuring I'd be too preoccupied to.

My hand slid into his hair as the other splayed strongly against the wall, barely taking the weight off my forehead as I almost lost the ability to keep myself standing. Drake's free arm wound around my stomach and took the majority of my weight.

"Holy shit," I breathed as he worked me expertly.

The coil deep in my stomach was tightening with a blossoming warmth and I knew I was close. My head rested back against him as he supported me and pleasured me like it was effortless.

As I felt the coil reach the end of its tension, my hand fisted in his hair and I bit my lip. His fingers slowed, only drawing out the feeling of pure ecstasy as it crashed over me. My whole body tensed in bliss until the initial force of it was over. I leant against him for a moment, then spun around in his arms.

I reached up and nipped his earlobe with my teeth as I ran my hand over the bulge in his pants. "Now it's your turn to behave," I told him.

He groaned and I slipped my hand into his pants and caressed him. His head tipped back and he closed his eyes.

I smirked as I knelt down, hooking my fingers in his pants and drawing them down with me. He obediently stepped out of them and I threw them to the corner of the room.

I ran my hand up and down his shaft, slowly, gently, then leant forward and took him in my mouth. His indrawn breath was sharp and I felt his muscles contract. It didn't take him long to relax and his hand gently alighted on the back on my head.

I sucked him, placing my hand at the base of his shaft I couldn't take in – I'd also learnt it prevented surprising accidental deep-throat – as he groaned softly. His hips rocked to my rhythm and, when I felt him getting close, I slid him out of my mouth. Just in time. He came, my name on his lips, inadvertently all over my chest. I stroked him softly as he rode it out, smiling.

"Well, that's fucking embarrassing," he huffed, drawing me to standing.

"So that's not a good example of your stamina," I teased, thinking that seemed about on par with my previous experience.

He wrapped his arms around me and pulled me close. "It's been a while, okay?"

I laughed as he buried his face in my neck and kissed me.

15
Drake

I could totally do this. I could pull it off. It was actually starting to feel like I could be with Wren and not, you know, be with Wren. In the Biblical sense.

Not having sex wasn't even that hard. There were plenty of ways to satisfy all urges without going that final step. All going to plan, I could see this thing out until the end days perfectly sated and keeping my wife happy.

We spent the next two weeks investigating everything but the homerun. I made sure I knew every inch of her. Intimately. Every curve. Every mountain. Every valley. I paid them all the utmost attention, nothing short of what they deserved. And she'd amazed me how well she'd repaid the favour. No one had known my body better. None had been able to elicit that sort of white-hot response in me. Not even the first succubus to walk creation had been able to please me so well. And she'd tried. Very hard.

When I wasn't working, Wren and I were together. Her eyes lit with that mischievous desire as soon as she saw me. It was something I felt deep in my soul and my cock.

On the occasions we were stuck with my father, or the boys thought they had things to do in our room – I felt bad kicking Kyle out constantly – she showed me how to actually enjoy Samba Sunday. I began not hating Music Mondays. I fought harder in Tussle Tuesdays. I kept her in bed during Waterboarding Wednesdays. I let my father dress me up for Tiki Thursdays. I did my best to protect her from the worst of Dad's Faustian Fridays. And I actually went to Shakespeare Saturdays to watch the devilbums acting their little hearts out, then getting annoyed with each other and just start fighting.

Even when there were witnesses, I found myself holding her hand, holding her close. We snuck kisses even when it was totally obvious. I'd thrown her against a wall a couple of times in the tunnels and almost forgotten I was in a room full of hellspawn watching my every move. I wasn't a stranger to sexual exploits with viewers, but Wren was all mine and I wasn't sharing any part of her.

When we were alone, we couldn't get enough of each other. As the son of the Lord of Hell, my sexual appetite was known to be pretty rampant. I was the literal definition of insatiable. But Wren had no problem keeping up with me. Every time I thought I'd exhausted her interest in me, she went to extraordinary lengths to prove me wrong. And it was only polite to reciprocate. I'd actually never had sex that frequently before her, and we hadn't even got that far.

My existence had never felt so right. Perfect wasn't something I'd ever associated with my reality, but it was a word I was fucking close to using.

Until it all came crashing down around me.

I was doing my usual wander around Hell, torturing some souls, checking on the rest, when my route took me past Cerberus' domain. It had been a while since I'd seen the dog who – let's be honest – was the most responsible for me kissing Wren in the first place. It gave me a strange sense of sentimentality towards him. So, I thought I'd go and check on him.

I didn't expect to find practically my whole family there.

Dad had his fiddle out, gallivanting around. Wren was dancing around Cerberus, holding Kyle's hands while his hooves rested on her feet. They were both smiling and laughing while Larry and the quartet sang for them all. Truman was tapping his hoof over by the wall. Ignacio was jerking around in his version of dancing. Even Esther was there and watching everything carefully.

But I couldn't take my eyes off Wren for long. She looked so carefree and relaxed. She looked like she belonged, and that she wanted to belong. It gave me this buoyant feeling in my chest I couldn't remember feeling before.

That was when it happened.

I laughed.

It was like a split-second chuckle. If that.

But the whole of Hell stood still.

Every inhabitant of Hell looked at me.

Cerberus' tail fell between his legs and all six ears dropped as he looked at me.

Larry fell out of the air into a crumpled heap on the cavern floor.

Kyle, Ignacio and even Truman cowered in a definitive 'oh no'.

My father almost fell over in surprise. His fiddle dropped to the floor with a twang.

Wren paused and looked at me in curiosity.

There were no screams or shrieks of eternal torment in any zone throughout the whole of my father's domain.

Hell was so silent you could have heard a cricket chirp on the surface.

All of that I might have been able to take.

But when I saw that Esther had cracked a knowing smile? That was when I knew shit had just got real.

Everything I'd told myself since I'd brought Wren to Hell was suddenly ash in my mouth. Every happy, light feeling I'd had crashed inside me. Every one of her smiles pierced through me like a thousand molten blades, searing flesh and muscle.

How had I let her become comfortable in Hell?

How had I let myself think it was all okay?

"Drake?" she asked, coming over to me.

I couldn't help it. I took her face in my hands and kissed her hard.

I felt her smile before she pulled away gently. It was there, in her eyes, as they searched mine. She could tell something was bothering me, but she didn't know what it was.

I hadn't known what it was.

I knew now.

I felt like a piece of me would cease to exist if I let her go home. But I was convinced I'd forfeit the right to see her smile, to touch her, if I let her stay. Maybe it was just going to be better to give in, to sleep with her, and let her go home. Never seeing her again would be far easier to endure than seeing her stuck in Hell for eternity and watching it eventually eat away at her.

"What's up?" she asked.

I heard Dad clear his throat unnecessarily loudly, then the music started up again as though he was giving us some privacy.

Grandad save this inability to lie. "Very little."

Her nose wrinkled in distaste. "Talk to me."

"There's nothing to talk about." There wasn't. My mind was made up. Even if it wasn't, I wasn't having a conversation about it with her.

She took my hand. "Do you want to dance with me? Or do you want some actual privacy and we can talk?"

I pressed my lips together. "I've still got a few more tortures to do."

She swung my hand coaxingly. "Hell won't stop because you take some time off. There are surely enough demons here to make sure everyone's properly tortured for the day."

She wasn't wrong. But I didn't want to talk. If we talked, I might say too much. If I said too much, one of two things happened; she reciprocated my sentiments, both good or bad, which meant she either wanted to go home or she didn't. Neither of which would give me any comfort. My feelings were hard enough without adding hers to the mix.

She leant up to my ear. "We don't have to talk…"

That I could do. That I wanted to do.

I suddenly felt like there was a looming deadline. I was running out of time with her and I had to spend as much time with her as possible.

Portent.

The tell-tale foreboding settled in me. The heartbeat that was threatening to quicken. The breath that didn't quite feel full. The anxious nervousness. The pricking at the back of my neck, begging me to turn around. The restlessness in my whole body.

It was worse than the day she wandered into Cerberus' domain. It was worse than the day my mother had died. It took everything in me not to spring into the air and go and goad Cadriel to beating the ever-hating shit out of me.

There was nothing I could do.

I knew what the portent heralded.

And I was as relieved as I was tormented by it.

"Drake?" Wren asked, uncertainty creeping into her voice.

I looked down at her, unable to muster even a ghost of a smile for her benefit. I hoped she'd understand.

"Bedroom," I ordered.

She didn't complain as I whisked her away to our room. I closed the door and locked it, ensuring no more unwelcome visitors could interrupt us. As soon as we had our privacy, I grabbed her dress and pulled her to me. Her lips found mine instantly and her hands made for my jeans button as I tried to lift her dress.

Wren laughed, but I was too focussed. I needed the feel of her around me. I needed her skin on mine. I needed to hear her moaning my name. I needed grounding. I felt like I was about to disintegrate into nothing, and she was my only anchor to creation.

We were undressed in no time. I picked her up and carried her to our bed. I threw her down and wasted no time climbing over her. She smiled up at me, her posture relaxed and easy. Her hair fanned out along the pillows. She was, put simply, perfection.

As I lowered myself over her, my heart caught.

This wasn't right.

I couldn't do it.

I wanted so badly to make her my wife unequivocally.

I felt like she wanted that too.

But we'd never even talk about what that meant.

"Do you know what marriage to me means, Wren?" I blurted out.

She frowned. "What do you mean."

"Do you know what it really means? To be my wife."

She shook her head. "I…don't know. I think so—"

"It means different things for us."

She was looking at me with that slightly spaced-out look I knew meant she was processing. So, I continued.

"Our marriage means I can never marry again while you live." A rule my father enjoyed breaking, but one I would be unable to. "It leaves you free to enter into a legal human marriage. If we were to consummate our marriage, it would become legal by all laws of Hell. It would be no more than that unless…" My voice failed me.

"Unless what?" she asked, her hand running over my back comfortingly.

I pulled myself together. "Unless you freely offer me your soul."

"Like…like some sort of pact or—?"

I shook my head. "No. But it is as binding."

"Oh. Okay."

"I just…wanted you to have all the facts."

She smiled. "Thank you."

I nodded curtly, not knowing what to say to that.

As she pulled me down to kiss her, I felt a little bit guilty.

I was unable to lie. But I could omit like a boss. And I'd conveniently left out the part where I would have to give her my soul in return. Telling her that would surely only result in an expectation for further explanation.

Which wasn't going to happen.

I couldn't risk the chance of revealing she already had mine.

16

Wren

When I woke up, I saw Drake watching me. I smiled as I stretched, and he ran his hand down my body.

"Morning," I said.

"Morning."

His voice was still… Cold wasn't quite the right word for it. But there had been something almost…heavy about it since the day before. He'd been fine in the morning, then I'd seen him in Cerberus' domain and it was like everything and nothing had changed. The night before had been different. No less amazing, but there was something about it that had my heart fluttering and words beginning with 'L' wander in to my head.

"Sleep well?" I asked as he kept looking at me.

"Enough."

"Is everything okay?" I looked him over.

"Just thinking."

"About what?"

"How much do you remember about our wedding?" he asked me.

I rolled to face him as I thought back. "I don't know. I think I *think* I remember more than I actually do. I remember you left just after, though."

He nodded. "I did."

Something hit me. "You said your mum died?"

Drake nodded. "She did."

"When?"

"When I was eight."

"I'm so sorry." I paused. "Is that why you left?"

He nodded vaguely. "It is what it is."

"How did she die?"

He watched as he laced his fingers with mine, then breathed out heavily before looking into my eyes. "My father sent Cadriel to kill her and collect me."

I felt my heart jerk painfully in my chest. "He…?" I breathed.

"My father's a stickler for propriety. I was a son of Hell and, as such, I belonged there. He was more than happy to remove whatever obstacles necessary to get what he wanted."

"And you…forgave him?"

Drake sighed. "More like I accepted the inevitable. And, back then, Dad kept a close eye on me, showering me with whatever flights of fancy he thought would buy the love of an eight-year-old boy and make up for the loss of a beloved parent."

"Did it work?"

His thumb ran over my hand. "It worked long enough to avoid the biting sting of her loss. By the time I fully comprehended my…life, her death was worn down to a dull ache in me."

"Do you still get to see her?"

He shook his head. "No," he scoffed.

"Why not?"

"She was killed by Grigori. That's like auto-entrance to Heaven in Samael's books."

"What does all that mean? What are Grigori? Cadriel's Grigori, right?"

"Right." His smile was soft. "There are two kinds of what humans consider Fallen Angels. Grigori were sent from Heaven to keep watch over Grandad's creation. But Samyeza was always a thirsty bastard and it wasn't long before they were consorting with humans, teaching them forbidden arts of the holy ones. They were confined to Earth until the end days for their so-called crimes, but they found their own ways to visit Hell."

"And the other kind? Were they the ones who followed your dad?"

Drake huffed a humourless laugh. "You could say all of them followed him. It's not really a cut and dry situation. There's a lot of interconnecting politics going on. They've found themselves in two sects since, I suppose. The Grigori and… The others are the Fallen who think they can earn their way back into Heaven. Azazel leads them and he's made it his mission to kill every Nephilim in existence. His nose couldn't be any further up Samael's arse. But Samyeza's boys give him a Heaven of a fight."

"Azazel or Samael?"

"Both, really. Samyeza's made it his mission – aside from fucking as many humans as possible – to protect Nephilim. Azazel wants to kill them. Samyeza's not too fussed if he takes one of Azazel's boys out of commission in the process of protecting them."

"Heaven and Hell are way more complicated than I realised."

Drake smiled at me. "They are. But you won't have to deal with any of that. When you die, you'll just get to spend your death in paradise."

"The wife of Lucifer's son isn't already bound for Hell?" I teased.

"Not technically my wife," he whispered and the mood shifted subtly.

What was a sombre and almost emotional aura became tinged with very visceral, delicious, sexual tension. I was hyper-aware of where Drake's hands were. I could feel his body even though it wasn't all touching me. My heart rate increased. My breathing got slower and deeper. My whole body hummed for his touch. Even though his touch would send me home, I felt like I needed it to keep breathing.

Whenever the subject came up, it seemed clear that I'd be leaving at some point. So maybe it was a good idea it was sooner rather than later. The longer I was in Hell, the more I felt for him and the more I was sure it was going to hurt when it inevitably came to an end – my restraint could only go so far, I knew I'd sleep with him at some point. He'd even brought it up the night before. So, why put off something we both wanted?

I trailed my fingers over his cheek. "I could be…"

I felt him tense as though he really was a part of me. He licked his bottom lip slowly as he searched my eyes. His breath seemed to have caught. His hand, his fingers still laced with mine, didn't move. His eyes had been red since we'd woken up, but they glowed fiercely now.

"You know what you're asking?" he rasped.

I nodded and wriggled forward to touch my nose to his. "I do."

As a sentence, it was simple. As a meaning, it was layered with intricacies I didn't think even he fully understood. But we both knew what I was saying, and he didn't need me to tell him twice.

He brought me close to him, still lying side-by-side, and looked into my eyes deeply before bringing my lips to his. It started out rather chaste and meaningful. It didn't stay that way for long.

My knee hugged Drake's hip, bringing us closer together. He ran his hand down it firmly, stopping only to grip my butt cheek and pull me closer.

I kissed him hard, cupping his cheek with my hand. When I nipped his lip, I felt him smile against me before he pushed me down and moved over me. He looked down at me with a truly sinful smirk, his eyes blazing red and igniting a fire deep in me. I didn't just want him. I needed him. All of him.

I brought my leg up to hug his hip again and his smirk grew. As he settled between my legs – feeling like he was born to be there – he kissed me. It was passionate, but softer and I melted beneath him. The feeling was intensified as his hand slid between us. His let his fingers glide over my clit and down to my opening with the promise of more that had me about to lose my mind.

"Fuck, you're wet," he murmured, nipping my lip.

I could only moan in response and I reached between us and took him in my hand.

"Tell me what you want," he commanded.

"You," I told him. "I want you."

I was not expecting the compassion of the kiss he gave me next, but it filled me up with a warmth that stoked the raging fire in my belly.

Drake took himself from me and lined himself up. His kiss didn't falter as he slowly slid into me with ever-deeper thrusts. He only paused when he was in to the hilt and I felt him pulsating inside me. We looked at each other for the space of a few steady heartbeats and I felt contented in a way I never had before. The rightness in it was clear to me, no matter what came next.

I took his cheek in my hand and brought his lips back to mine as I rolled my hips against him. He groaned. His hand went to my hip, coaxing my leg further up and letting him thrust deeper.

His movement was slow and steady. A pulsating rhythm that I felt deep in my soul, connecting us in the most primal way. Every long thrust intensified, tightening the coil low in my stomach. The arm that wasn't holding him up was constantly exploring, ranging over my body like he was committing it to memory. His lips rarely left mine, but when they did it was only to cross my cheek and down to my neck, sometimes as far as my collarbone before he dragged his nose over me to kiss me passionately again.

I felt cared for. I felt understood. I felt loved.

As that coil tightened, sending little pulses of pleasure, my breathing became more ragged, my sighs became moans and our pace increased. Each thrust was as long and steady, but faster and faster until something in me snapped, spinning me into a daze of bursting sensuality and pure carnal pleasure.

Drake slowed as I caught my breath, giving me a smile that would make his father blush. But once my breath was back, the only description I had for it was he totally drilled me. Zings of electricity – aftershocks of my orgasm – shot through me pleasantly with each stroke. And when I finally thought I wasn't going to be able to take anymore, he slowed again. His hips rolled deep and steady and I felt it all building to a crescendo once more.

His head fell to my shoulder and he let out a long, soft groan and I came again. He throbbed inside me, hot and hard. I felt an invigorating mix of totally energised and like cooked spaghetti.

"Oh, my God," I laughed under my breath, throwing my arm over my eyes.

"Bringing up my grandfather? Sure way to kill the mood."

I chuckled. "I'm sorry. But that was…" I blew out heavily, having no words for it.

"Oh," he said with a cocky smirk. "You enjoyed it?"

I laughed. "I think I felt my soul leave my body at one point." It was only partially a joke.

He buried his nose in my neck. "We can't have that. I'll have to try to be less than amazing next time."

He looked up and we gazed into each other's eyes. We both felt it. We both knew. Whatever the depth of feelings we had for each other, it was all coming to an end. Our marriage was consummated. We were officially married under the rules of Hell.

It was only a matter of how long it would be before I was sent me home.

Turns out it was sooner than I expected.

17

Drake

Some would call me weak for giving in. Some would say I was weak for not having her sooner.

I'd call them all arseholes and tell them to fuck right off.

It hadn't taken long for Dad to know our marriage had been consummated. As in seconds. I was still inside her.

There was a 'Congratulations' banner and confetti to celebrate. Appearing over us as I kissed her, I got glitter in my hair as she laughed and covered her face with her hands.

I was dressed and flying to Dad's throne room in moments, Wren running after me and begging me to slow down. I threw open the doors and pointed my finger at him as I landed.

"One thing!" I yelled at him as I stalked towards him. "One thing in my life. That's all I ask. One thing that's mine. That doesn't have your stench all over it as you poke your bedazzled nose where it's not wanted!"

"Ah, here's the man of the hour," he said, turning from whatever, he was cooking up on his Planning Table now. "Over a month of waiting? How was it?"

"None of your business!"

"Drake…" Wren said, finally catching up to me.

"Here she is!" Dad cried happily. His face fell into an exaggerated frown, he snapped his heels together, and he clapped his hands together in front of what looked like a safari suit. "Well, a deal's a deal."

"Wait. What?" I looked around.

"I was promised one daughter-in-law. Serenity was promised a one-way trip home. She held up her end of the bargain. It's time I hold up mine."

He held his hand up and I stepped forward. "Dad!"

The devil looked at me expectantly. "Yes?"

"At least let her pack her things."

I had to be imagining the look of disappointment on his face, as momentary as it was. He sighed heavily and rolled his eyes. "Fine. Of course."

"No! No! No!" Kyle came skidding into the room and latched himself to Wren's legs.

Ignacio came hurtling along behind him while Truman huffed less stately than usual behind Ignacio.

"Kyle," Dad said fondly. "We made a deal. Serenity must go home." Here, Dad looked at me oddly, but again it was only momentary. "If she didn't, we'd be breaking a deal. And what do we say about breaking deals?"

"Not allowed," Kyle said sullenly, still wrapped around Wren's legs.

"Might I offer a...negotiation, sirs?" Truman asked, stepping forward.

Dad dropped into his throne and laced his fingers over his stomach. "What have you got?"

"If Miss Serenity must go home, at least let us go with her, sir."

Dad unlaced everything and sat forward. "Sorry. You... The three of you?"

Truman nodded, taking another couple of hesitant steps towards my father. Ignacio had his back. And I'm sure Kyle would have if he wasn't busy loudly sobbing on Wren.

"Yes, sir." Truman coughed. "Ignacio, Kyle and I."

At the sound of his name, Kyle looked over, still sniffling and tears streaming down his little red face. "Kyle go?" he pleaded.

"The three of you would abandon your post with your master, the prince of Hell, and go to live on Earth with Serenity?" Dad asked and I could see he was almost sold.

"We'll take care of her," Ignacio growled.

"Drake…" Wren hissed and I looked at her.

I couldn't quite understand what she was trying to tell me. I almost dipped into her mind, but plausible deniability was a wonderful invention.

"What say you, son?" Dad called to get my attention again.

I looked at him. "About the boys going?"

"Yes." Dad nodded. "Do you think you can do without them for the rest of Serenity's life?"

I did not want to think about her death so my, "Yes," came out rather strangled.

"And you trust them on Earth? Trust they can take care of her?"

I swallowed hard. "They are loyal to Wren. They'll take care of her as well as anyone."

"No!" Wren cried, stumbling as she tried to walk to me with Kyle still attached to her legs. "No, I don't–"

Dad stood up with a flourish. "Then it's all settled. Boys, go and help Serenity pack. And get anything you might want to take with you."

I felt the argument on the tip of my tongue. Everything in me screamed to find a way to keep her. I wanted to tell my father that the deal had changed. But if I found a way for her to stay with me, I was condemning her to millennia in Hell while her friends and family aged and died.

"Truman," I snapped. "Go."

Truman trotted over to her and took her hand. "Come, ma'am. Let's get you all sorted out."

There were tears in Wren's eyes, but her face was set in a fierce anger. I didn't blame her. I wanted more time with her. But it was better this way. This way gave her a chance to live a life. A life I could never give her no matter how much I wanted to.

Even though I loved her, I had to let her go back. Though, perhaps it was because I loved her.

I gave Wren nothing in response. I couldn't afford to.

Finally, with a look of hatred shot at my father, she let Truman lead her out. Ignacio managed to pry Kyle off her legs, but he went running after her and demanded to hold her other hand.

The doors crashed shut behind them with the epic boom of finality.

"Well, that took longer than I expected," Dad said, trotting over to his planning table and picking up a piece, apparently wondering where to put it back. "I commend her restraint. That girl put up a Heaven of a fight. Shame she can't stay."

I glared at him. "You got what you wanted."

He looked at me. "Did I *really*, though?"

"You wanted me married. I'm married. What more did you want?"

Dad crossed his arms. "You know what, Drake. If you don't know the answer to that, you can go and spend the rest of eternity thinking about it. You're not too old for a timeout!"

I growled in frustration. "I am definitely too old for a timeout. You want to try it? I'll–"

Dad grew about three times his usual size. It was all flame and anger and horns. "Do not test me, son." His voice was low and gravelly and echoed around the room, and even the guard demons ran in terror. He shrunk back to his normal self, in a suit this time, and brushed his hair back into place. "Now look at what you made me do. I've gone and lost my temper."

I wanted to show him what a loss of temper really looked like. I wanted to try out my own rage-monster and feel the gratification of scaring every creature in creation. I needed to feel powerful, to combat some of the weakness I'd felt as soon as Wren had walked out of the room.

Dad was smirking at me knowingly. He knew what was going through my head. He knew what I was feeling. He knew what I was thinking. He knew it all. They called Grandad omniscient? He'd passed more than a little of that on. Especially when it came to sins. And I was feeling pretty much every one of them.

My father was waiting for me to do something. He was waiting to see what I'd end up choosing. He had an idea of what my reaction would be, but he was looking forward to whatever the actual result.

The result was I screamed at him and stormed out of his throne room.

I needed to clear my head. I needed pain. I needed focus.

I barrelled my way through Hell, woe to any creature I came across, lost in my thoughts and mental anguish.

I'd done the right thing. I'd done what was best for Wren and saved the consequences for me.

So why did it feel so wrong?

A guard demon stepped in front of me, holding his pike in the most unthreatening manner I think I'd ever seen.

"Uh…" He cleared his throat. "His devilness would be quite pleased if you could restrict your tantrum to the zones currently experiencing downtime and to please stop getting in the way of the smooth running of the whole operation. Souls like to be tortured in peace, you know."

I heard my father's voice in the message. Which wasn't surprising, guard demons were very good at remembering messages in the short-term and would basically recite them verbatim to the intended recipient.

"You can tell my father to go fuck him—"

"I suspect he's tried that one out already," came a voice.

I turned to Cadriel. Just the angel I needed.

"Did Daddy send you to put me down?" I sneered.

"*Daddy* thought you needed a healthy outlet for your frustrations now that that pretty little human won't—"

I crashed into him and sent us both falling. His wings erupted and he propelled us upwards.

"Thank you, sir!" the guard demon called.

"You don't talk about her," I told Cadriel as we circled each other mid-flight.

"Me? I wasn't talking about anyone."

The Grigori? They got to lie. The benefits of being Fallen.

My father, while cast out of Heaven, was never spurned by Grandad. That was a big difference. Dad was just in creation's longest timeout while Grandad used him to do all the less-savoury jobs in the afterlife.

I envied the Grigori their silver tongues and their lack of emotion.

"Had I been talking about anyone, I might have wondered how such a pretty little human is going to survive on Earth now."

He was goading me and I was more than happy to let him.

We fought. One of our most vicious in all of history.

Cadriel's favoured weapon was the double-handed axe. It stood easily as tall as him, the head reaching at least half his wingspan. And he twirled it like it was plastic straw. To us, it was. We had the might of Grandad behind us, built into our very fabric so finely that even he couldn't unravel it.

And still I let too many blows hit me.

Hit was a generous word for the damage he dealt.

Every swing of Cadriel's axe crashed into me with the force of a ten-tonne truck. Every time a blade touched me, it rent my flesh almost to the bone. Normally, my healing process wasn't quite so quick, but I was going what the Grigori called supernova.

Nephilim are inherently more powerful than angels – we're a combination of Grandad's favourite sons and each part makes us stronger. This wasn't news. But every now and then, a Nephilim went supernova. Some emotion riled them up to the point there was too much power in them for their bodies to contain. It had to come out other ways. Accelerated healing. Heightened speed and senses. More strength.

This worked in my favour twofold.

While my wounds healed almost as quickly as Cadriel could deal them, I felt each one tenfold. And each one settled me. It would be a stretch to call the raging storm calmed. But the intensity of my impulsive anger was dulled a little.

"Are you so worried about the pretty little human that you'd let her send you supernova?" Cadriel provoked.

My head was on just straight enough to answer him. "She'll be fine. The boys went with her. Each one of them would die for her."

"And if Azazel sends one of his errand boys to kill the Nephilim bastard's wife?" Cadriel asked, all nonchalance.

I hadn't thought of that. The suggestion took me off guard and, while I took that in – with the added imagery of Azazel himself running her through playing out in my mind – he punched me full force in the gut.

Cadriel grabbed me to keep me from falling as I choked for breath and whispered almost reverently in my ear, "Even Ignacio can't stand up against one of those Fallen bastards."

I pushed him away forcefully. "If I go up there, she'd be more of a target."

"Didn't stop you the first time."

"We weren't technically married the first time."

"You know Azazel's determined to kill you. You're Lucifer's last."

"He knows what my father would do to him."

Cadriel nodded. "So, next best thing. He can't rip your heart out literally, he'll do it figuratively."

"Have I been going too easy on you today?" I growled, feeling my anger start to grow restless again.

Cadriel grinned. "I could protect her."

"Oh, no." I pointed at him. "I know what you're like. Humans are like catnip to Grigori. You don't go near her."

"You'd risk her life rather than have me protect her?"

I twirled my sword in my hand. "She'll be fine." I had to believe it. "They'd have to find her first."

"I always said Lucifer's bastard son was incapable of love."

I roared in anger. My wings burst forth, driving me into him. I slammed him against the wall, my sword buried deep in his stomach.

"Tainted," Cadriel taunted me.

I twisted the sword and he laughed as he grimaced in pain.

"You keep goading me and my father will think you have less than my safety in mind," I told him.

Blood burbled out of his mouth as he grinned. "Perhaps my reminding you of your destiny *is* having your safety in mind?" he spat. "Whether the Fallen kill her, whether the potestas get to her first, she'll still die, Morningstar. She's mortal."

I didn't want to hear it, but it was true.

We were all slaves to our destiny no matter what path we took or where we ended up.

Damned slaves.

We were damned if we did, and still damned if we didn't.

18
Wren

Going back to a human life was difficult. It wasn't just feeling like a piece of myself was missing. It wasn't just the relative coldness. It wasn't just the fact that I was surrounded by the mundane again. It was also the boys.

The presence of Truman, Ignacio and Kyle gave me equal amounts of solace and sadness. And they knew it. Truman kept most of his more sardonic comments to himself. Kyle fixed himself by my side as often as he could. And Ignacio had taken to scouting for every and any threat I might face on a daily basis. This led to more than one accident.

The blender had been replaced twice already because I'd managed to let it explode in my face and Ignacio wasn't going to let some mechanical beast vomit its guts on me.

Mrs Finster's cat had dared to hiss at me as I walked inside one afternoon and Ignacio had scared it so badly it had run too quickly inside and broken its own leg.

He'd bitten clean through the pipe of the vacuum cleaner because I somehow vacuumed up my own earring.

My computer was running too slowly for my fragile mood and I'd whacked it in annoyance so Ignacio threw it out the window.

He'd taken an interesting liking to Dad and could occasionally be distracted by following him around the house. Dad had taken a couple of days to get used to this behaviour, but actually quite enjoyed having a devilbum shadow after a week.

Kyle was besotted with Harmony. He was always agitated when I took too long to get ready for school, wanting to go downstairs and watch out the window for her car. And could always be found at the window when I walked in the front door.

When he wasn't on Harmony-watch, he was busy investigating – and tasting – everything Earth had to offer. His favourite discovery was Whizz Fizz sherbet. Anytime he ate it, it made his ears flap and his eyes blink rapidly while his tongue stuck out and he made a little high-pitched whining noise.

In between those two strenuous pastimes, he could be found with his nose pressed against the TV as he tried to lick whatever was on it. He particularly liked the ABC kid's shows with the songs and the colours. As he went about whatever else he was getting up to, he almost always sang one of those songs.

Truman was…Truman. As the most level-headed of the three of them, he appointed himself my 'out of the house' guardian. He could apparently appear invisible to whoever he wanted, so he came to school with me, following me around with his stately trot in complete silence.

Harmony had been surprised, to say the least, when I arrived back home with three devilbums and claiming I was married to Lucifer's son.

"Hang on," she'd said, shaking her head as Kyle batted her hip to get her attention. "Try that on me one more time."

"I…" Grunting in frustration, I pulled the photo off my bed where it had fallen. I showed it to her and she shrugged.

"Huh?"

I sighed. "Hot guy next door?"

"Yum. Remember him."

"That was Drake." I held the picture up again and she looked between us in confusion.

I saw the moment the lightbulb went off. "Oh. Oh!" she breathed. "As in, Drake?"

I nodded. "He came to collect me as his wife, to Hell."

Harmony pointed at Kyle. "I'm finding it hard to think you're crazy at this point."

"Kyle's…enthusiastic." I waved that away. "No. Look, I was gone two days here. But it was over a month there. Over a month."

"Of being stuck in Hell with Super Hotty." Harmony's eyebrows waggled cheekily. "Huh? Huh?"

I couldn't stop my smile.

She pointed at me with a victorious smile. "Oh, my God. I knew it! He's amazing, isn't he?"

I bit my lip as I nodded. "Yeah."

"Yeah," she giggled and I joined her.

Then I was batting her. "Not the point!"

"Why? *Was* he a bit wet?"

"He wasn't the wet one–"

"Oh, hello!"

I snorted. "Stop distracting me!"

She shrugged as she took the flower Kyle had brought her. "You fell in love with him."

"What?"

"What?"

"I–"

"Fell in love with the devil's son. So, what?"

I blinked. "I did not fall in love with the… I'm too young to be in love, let alone married!"

"Sounds like you're not when you're stuck in a timeless sauna," she sang.

"Can you–?"

"Not let you deny it? Yup."

"Harm! I'm barely eighteen."

"And yet you're married. Ugh. And I missed *both* weddings. Although, I'm kind of glad I wasn't at the second. Did it even count as a wedding, really? When are you going back?"

I blinked. "What?"

"When are you going back to him? Or is he coming here?" She'd looked at me in total excitement. "Are we going to have a proper wedding? Am I going to be a bridesmaid? Of course, I am. Can I wear flats, though?"

She wasn't the only one who seemed to think I was irrevocably in love with Drake. Neither was she the only who seemed to have it in her head that either I was going back to Hell or Drake was coming to Earth. And everyone seemed to think another wedding was in order!

"Are you sure it's over, dear?" Mum asked while stirring dinner a full ten days after I'd come home.

I sighed. "Yes."

"What a shame."

"What? Why?"

"Oh, you've only been a beacon of joy since you got back," Tilly said sarcastically, leaning on the kitchen bench.

Mum nodded. "Well, yes. She's sad. But–"

"But what?" I asked.

"Well, I was just thinking… We could have had a proper wedding. If it wasn't over."

"A proper wedding?" Tilly exclaimed. I couldn't tell if she thought it was a great idea or a terrible idea.

Mum nodded again. "Traditional. Church. White dress. All our family and friends. It would have been lovely."

"Can they even enter a church?" Tilly mused as I said, "Mum, I'm barely eighteen!"

Why did I have to keep reminding people?

"Eighteen or eighty," Mum chided. "You're in love with him."

"How do you know I won't grow out of it? Or that he made me fall in love with him?"

"Because we didn't raise you to go losing your head, magical powers or not." She looked me over meaningfully and I rose my eyebrow in question.

"What?" I asked.

"I didn't notice you denying it."

"So?" I was on the defensive.

"So, what use has Drake got to make you in love with him now? If it wasn't real, would you still feel it?"

Well, I knew it was real. But, how did they?

"Are you really the *most* upset about not having a real wedding?" Tilly asked, leaning her chin in her hands.

Mum smiled softly. "A parents' truest dream is to see their children happy. If that can include a wedding, then all the better."

"What if I don't want to get married?" my sister challenged.

Mum's smile grew more rueful. "Then you'll have broken your mother's heart," she joked.

"Would a real wedding really mean that much?" I asked.

I was thinking about that. I was thinking about doing the whole big wedding thing. Me in a white dress. Drake waiting for me at the end of the aisle. A minister. A church full of family and friends and Lucifer and hellspawn. I wasn't quite sure how it would work. I doubted it could work. But there was a small part of me that didn't want to take the possibility off the board.

Mum looked at me. "Think of what Mrs Finster will say if she found out my Serenity was marrying the devil's son." It was meant in jest to break my dismal mood, but it had the opposite effect.

I didn't want her to see that though, so I smiled. "She'd have gossip for years."

"And green as a cucumber with jealousy," Mum chuckled.

I nodded. "I'm just going to…" I pointed behind me with no real intention or desire to be anywhere other than not there anymore.

Well, that wasn't strictly true.

There was only one place I really wanted to be.

I couldn't do it. I couldn't live a human life anymore. I couldn't leave it all totally behind, but life without Drake was Hell on Earth. And if I was living in Hell, then I may as well actually be in Hell with the man I loved. My head had spent enough time arguing I was too young to be in love, let alone a wife, but I was done listening. No one else had been anyway and my heart told me otherwise. It was time to follow it, even to Hell.

"Truman?" I asked as I jogged into my room.

Truman was folding my laundry. Kyle was dressed in my old Belle costume – I guess I'd always had a thing for falling in love with moody kidnappers – and having a tea party with my old teddy bears. For some reason, I hadn't been able to look at them the same since I'd got back and was more than happy for him to have them. And Ignacio was glaring out the window like he was on the lookout for threats, which was sweet in his own way.

"Yes, ma'am?"

"How would one get into Hell?"

"Suicide is always the quickest way," Ignacio offered as he squashed his face against my window as if he'd seen something.

"Uh…good to know. What about…without dying?"

"Gates!" Kyle squeaked as he dropped imaginary sugar cubes in Abbit's cup.

"Gates?" I looked to Truman, who was likely to give me the most comprehensible response.

"Indeed, ma'am. The gates would be a human's best way in."

"Best?" I clarified, not liking the way that sounded.

"Yes, ma'am. A human entering Hell, without some help, would have very little chance of getting into Hell unscathed. First, they would have to find a gate and survive the harrowing encounter with the gatekeeper. If they passed and made it through the welcome flames, they would still have to contend with Cerberus, who has strict instructions not to let any being in or out of Hell without his master's explicit permission."

I knew his speech was designed to remind me of the very real dangers. It would put off any normal person from willy-nilly deciding on a jaunt down to Hell. But I wasn't just anyone. It still sounded bad but, if all I had was a best shot, I'd take it.

"So, it would take a remarkable human to make their way into Hell?"

Truman nodded thoughtfully. "Without extraordinary circumstances or some measure of Cerberus' regard, it would be almost impossible for even a remarkable human. Though many would say those qualities would only be granted to a human already exceptionally remarkable."

I smiled at his compliment, but wasn't going to get distracted by it. "I don't suppose devilbums know of any gates?"

"If a human had the determination to enter Hell of his or her own volition, then I would be happy to show them the way."

"Kyle also! Kyle also," he said, nodding vigorously.

"I'm not keeping my mistress from her husband," Ignacio grunted.

I looked at them all and breathed out carefully. "Okay. Let's go to Hell, boys."

19
Drake

It had been months by my reckoning. Maybe a week by hers.

In all the eons I'd survived in Hell, no time had felt slower. Millenia of torture, of collection, the endless monotony of the heat and the screams and the fucking souls, and this is what got to me. This absence.

I hadn't felt such a loss when my mother had died. But back then, my father had thrown every bauble and shiny toy and voluptuous woman at me a guy could handle. He'd made it his duty to keep me distracted and entertained. Most of it was for his own amusement. I'd been a new audience for his latest performances. But a small part of me had believed it was because he didn't know how else to be fatherly.

I'd long since grown out of even pretending to mollify his exploits, but that didn't stop him falling back into old habits.

I walked into his throne room to find it darker than usual. I was so lost in my own world that I didn't see what was coming next. Even though it wasn't the first time in the last few months.

Opening bars rumbled out and a spotlight swung up to illuminate him standing on his throne. He wore a top hat, pushed low over his eyes. He wore one of his sparkliest suits, the sequins creating a blinding glare as the spotlight moved slowly over them.

"What are you–?" My voice cut out with a hand from him.

The song started out slow and low. It was mournful and capable of tugging a heart as cold as mine. There was true emotion in my father's voice as the vocals rose in volume. It wasn't a song that existed on earth. This was a Lucifer original, a song about loss and love and the inescapable marching of time. It was gut-wrenching. I felt my heart constrict in my chest, my throat got tight and hot.

Just as I was going to go over there and physically rip him a new one, it all changed.

The tempo switched. The lights went from the single spotlight to bright and garish and, as he rolled his top hat along his arms and shoulders from one hand to the other, his suit changed into something you saw in a kitsch Hawaiian hotel; white pants, a tropical shirt, a couple of leis, and even a ukulele. There were even violently bursting tiki torches and a tiny volcano that was dancing along with the tune as it shot spurts of lava into the air.

"So, you're all alone and now she's gone," was a line that sent me over the edge of mild annoyance and into heavy-duty anger.

My wings sprouted and I charged him, pinning him to the floor with my hand over his throat. The show stopped abruptly and he looked up at me mock-innocently.

"Was it something I said?" he squeaked, batting his eyes.

"You think?" I snapped, pushing myself to standing.

"If I could make a *small* observation…?"

I rolled my neck. "Can I stop you?"

"In the eons you've lived here, I've only ever seen your wings on Tussle Tuesdays. Easier to keep up with Cadriel that way, but…"

"What's your point?"

"Well, only that it seems, whenever Serenity is involved, your first instinct is wings."

I frowned at him. "I don't…" I shifted uncomfortably. "It is not."

"I just…" he cleared his throat loudly. "Well, the promise has been fulfilled. The bargain struck and kept. She went home. No one said how long she had to stay there." He shrugged suggestively.

"She's better off on Earth."

"Is she?"

My gaze narrowed. "What do you know?"

He settled into what he considered his teaching mode. He completed it with a cardigan and spectacles. "Son, I was the first to sin. So says Daddy, anyway. I've spent quite literally the whole of time witnessing love in all its forms. Or lack thereof. It's not in my nature for such things to affect me. But, as your father," He pushed the glasses up his nose, "I feel obliged to tell you that you're in love with her."

My eyebrow rose of its own accord. "Nah. You think?"

Dad opened and closed his mouth a couple of times. "You know?"

I threw up my arms in frustration. "Of course, I know!"

"Then why in Hell's name did you let me send her home? I thought you wanted her gone. I gave you ample opportunity to butt in. Why did you not fight tooth and nail to–?"

"Because she doesn't deserve to spend the rest of time here! She deserves a life. She deserves a good life and a good death and a chance to spend the rest of eternity in paradise."

"Oh, I see…" he said softly.

"You see what?" I asked.

He nodded knowingly. "No. Yes. I see. If you love her…"

"Enough riddles, old man."

"Set her free…" he finished. He looked up at me with a grin. "Clever boy."

I had no idea what he was talking about. "What?"

"Oh, you clever, sly, boy. If I'd ever had cause to doubt your parentage, this proves it. You can only be mine."

"What proves it?" I yelled. "Not the wings? Not the immortality? Not the ability to bend hellspawn to my will? Not the whole portent deal? Not even my propensity for torture?"

Dad shook his head as he came over to me. He put his hands on my shoulders with a wide smile. "If you love her, set her free. If she's yours, she'll return to thee."

I shrugged him off. "She's not coming back. And I'm not going to get her."

"Why? What did you tell her?"

I sighed. "I didn't tell her anything."

He smacked up upside the head. "Stupid boy!"

"What?"

"She went home believing you felt nothing for her?"

"What was I supposed to do?"

"Spend eternity in a love-filled marriage!" he cried like it was obvious.

165

"Excuse me if I don't take marital advice from a man with multiple failed marriages, will you?"

"I thought we'd covered this? Children don't get to meddle in the affairs of their parents."

"Well, 'affairs' is certainly the perfect word for it."

He sighed deeply. "You do not know how I regret the traits you inherited from your mother."

"Can you, just once, keep your scathing comments about her to yourself?"

"That was not meant as a slight, son," he said quietly. "Your life would be easier if you only took after me. But you are half-human, and destined to feel with the heart of a human no matter how much you try to harden yourself. Its's just the way it is. I would give anything to change that, to make your existence easier, but even your grandfather cannot."

I took a second to get my head around that, around the moment we seemed to be having. It was the most intimate conversation we'd ever had. It was the only time in my entire existence I could remember him openly showing me even a hint of affection or attachment. Hot on the heels of Wren's loss, I wasn't sure I could take it. It was too much emotion for a heart that had felt nothing for too long.

"Don't," I choked out.

"Don't what?" Dad asked.

"Don't start with that now."

"I'm not starting anything. I…" He cleared his throat. "I'm merely taking a minute to…try to help my son."

"Can you not?"

"Well, I'd much prefer not. All this emotion is…unseemly."

"And don't start with that."

He raised his hands innocently. "Not starting anything."

I nodded once. "Good."

"So… What's on the cards? Some more personal torture? Put some more work into the Millennial Meme Field? Or are you just going to go and mope in your room?"

I was going to go and mope in my room. Not that I was going to admit it out loud. But I didn't need to, because I'd got my mind-reading powers from somewhere. Or someone. That someone knew the answer, and knew what I thought about him knowing the answer.

"Uh huh," he huffed. "And that room you did up just for her is going to go untouched until the end days, is it?"

"Maybe," I sulked.

When I'd first brought Wren back, I'd had no idea how things would go. I'd had no idea that we'd have to actually be together before the marriage was official. So, I'd made up a room for us to share, leaving my room available if I'd needed – or wanted – a space of my own for…my own stuff. Okay, it was sex stuff. Sex with not her.

If I'd known what Wren was like, if I'd known how she'd make me feel, if I'd known we'd have to sleep together, I would have just had her in my room. But I hadn't and, despite the fact our room felt more like mine that my previous room, I hadn't been able to bring myself to going back in it since she left.

Neville stood watch outside it day and night, making sure no one went in there and disturbed it. I wanted it left the way she had. Especially after our last night and morning together. Aside from the glitter and the immediately following events, it had been perfect.

"What do you care anyway?" I snapped. "Your torture rate is up like six hundred percent. More blood. More pain.

More wretched despair. Hell has never been such a well-oiled machine. I'd have thought you'd be pleased!"

"Pleased?" he scoffed. "Really. What am I? A monster?" He looked at me pointedly and he turned into a literal monster. "Don't answer that."

I shook my head. "I'm not in the mood for your shit right now."

He deflated, literally like an inflatable Frankenstein, but didn't say anything as I turned and left the room.

"Afternoon, Master Drake," Neville said as I inadvertently passed him.

I paused and looked at the door above his head.

"Want me to open it up for you, sir?"

I almost took a step towards it. I almost nodded. The smell of her was becoming a distant memory I was clinging to like a man drowning. But I wasn't going to become one of those men who hung onto pieces of her in desperation. I didn't need to wallow in my agony, I needed to use it to strengthen myself.

Cadriel was on Earth on an errand for Samyeza.

So, if experiencing blinding pain wasn't available to take my mind off her, inflicting it was going to have to do.

"Thanks, Neville. I've got to see a bloke about some torture."

"Anytime, sir. Have an infernal day."

"Yeah, you too."

20

Wren

"This way. This way," Kyle called as he disappeared around a bend.

Truman hung between Kyle and me as though he wasn't sure who needed more protection. He threw the occasional look back at me

Ignacio, though, seemed to think for once that Kyle could handle whatever we came up against better than me. He stuck close by my side. His ears twitched this way and that as though he was constantly on alert.

After all I'd been through in the past month, after everything I'd seen, it was nice to know I could still be totally freaked out by the unknown. Except, I think most of my panic was at the idea of seeing Drake again rather than being concerned about what hellspawn we'd meet along the way.

It hadn't taken me long to convince the devilbums to show me the closest gateway back into Hell. It had still taken us a bit of time to get there and Harmony had demanded to drive us. Although, driving anywhere long-distance with three devilbums in the backseat was a whole new experience. I was pretty sure I knew how parents felt on road trips.

So, Harmony was on her way back home again and the boys and I were looking for the gateway into Hell. Because, like any sane, rational person, I was choosing to go back to Hell. I felt very Ancient Greek, just significantly lacking in the quest department.

I finally got around the bend and saw Kyle bouncing next to a rock wall that abruptly cut off what barely counted as a path.

Ignacio grunted and looked around, holding his makeshift spear in his claws tightly.

"We go in, ma'am," Truman said.

"In?" I clarified.

"There's a fissure here."

He held back the vines and I ducked to slip between the rocks where he pointed. Kyle took my hand gently, his claws cool and hard against my skin, and tugged me forward. My eyes took a while to adjust. But, as they did, I saw we walked into a large cavern.

The floor was impossibly smooth, meeting the bottom of the jagged walls as they arched up and over us many feet above. There was another fissure at the other end, through which I could see the flickering of flames that was both unnerving and tantalising. I could just hear the familiar soundtrack of Hell – faint screaming, but nothing too horrifying so as not to overly scare the tourists.

"This way, ma'am," Truman said softly.

The four of us took tentative steps forward, even Ignacio who was almost always the first one into the fray. As we got closer to the fissure, the dull sound of bells thundered through the cavern like some perverted shop bell. I also saw there was a shadowy form at the base of the fissure.

The form was a large stone throne and on the throne was a girl who looked barely older than me. She was sitting sideways; her back against one arm rest and her legs over the other. She had dark purple hair, pulled up into a style that looked centuries out of fashion. But she wore jeans and a hoodie like it was totally normal. I couldn't quite see what was in her hands, but she was staring at it.

As we neared the base of the throne, something caught on my foot and a small stone scattered away.

The girl looked up sharply, her eyes glowing bright yellow in the semi-darkness. She looked around, taking everything in in the space of a heartbeat. She stood up slowly, looking regal and authoritative.

"Speak," her voice boomed around the cavern.

"Miss Grace," Truman started, stepping forward.

But she cut him off. "Human. Speak."

I looked down at the devilbums, but they pushed me forward encouragingly. I swallowed hard, not sure why I was feeling so nervous.

"I… Um, hi," I started lamely.

"What brings you to this gate, human?"

"I… Well, I need to get into Hell."

She looked me over. "What business have the living in the afterlife?"

"It's…kind of personal."

"Any living who wish to pass through these gates must answer to the gatekeeper. That you have captured three of Hell's creatures will not help you."

I looked at the boys, who had implied this was going to be a lot easier than this.

Suddenly, the girl laughed and I looked back to see her jogging down the throne's stairs. "Sorry." She waved her hand at me as she stopped. "Sorry, I couldn't help myself. Of course, I know who you are. Oh, my Lucifer! Truman, it's actually her!"

"Ma'am, might I introduce Miss Grace, the gatekeeper," Truman said.

I looked between them, wondering why it was taking me so long to reconcile what I was seeing. "Miss Grace?"

"Grace, please, Mrs Morningstar."

Oh, I had so many feelings upon hearing that. "Call me Wren," I choked out.

"It is so wonderful to meet you, Wren. I would have come to see you earlier, but I'm kind of stuck here until the end of time, you see." Grace seemed overly enthusiastic about that.

I nodded. "Uh, no. Sure. Uh…why?"

"Oh. It's my punishment." She pointed to the fiery gash in the rock behind her. "Eternity as a gatekeeper."

"Eternity."

She nodded. "Yeah. But, as you know, time's a loose construct down here."

I could only nod again. "Of course."

Grace grinned and stepped back. "Right. So, on you go then. All public gates lead to Cerberus, mind. He's kind of a necessary good."

"Ma'am, we really should go," Truman said.

"Good luck!" Grace said as the devilbums started ushering me towards the gate.

I waved to Grace awkwardly as I steeled myself. I didn't have time to finish taking a breath as the boys gave me an encouraging hug and I felt the literal flames of Hell lick me as I passed through the gate.

I fell to all fours on the other side and heard the great big bark from all three of Cerberus' heads. The chorus sounded partial warning and partial greeting. Knowing Cerberus, he could be in any sort of mood to see me.

"Hey, Cerb," I coughed.

Ignacio helped me up as I heard Kyle running to the "Puppy!"

Cerberus barked again, a wave of semi-rancid breath washing over me. I looked up at him and smiled uncertainly. Rocky and Todd were baring their teeth at me, but Huxley looked a little confused.

"I need to see Drake, Cerberus. Will you let me pass?"

All three heads cocked to the side and he plonked his great big butt on the ground.

"I know. I cocked up. I never should have left. That's why I need to see him."

Rocky snapped at me, his jaws closing inches from my face. But I was Lucifer's daughter-in-law for Hell's sake, and I wasn't about to let Cerberus intimidate me from my husband.

I drew myself up to my tallest, which did nothing against the mammoth size of the hellhound. "I *will* see Drake, Cerberus. I do not need your permission."

Rocky huffed, but I could see Todd and Huxley were on my side. Todd was even grinning as best as his doggy mouth allowed.

"Step aside, Cerberus," I said in my most commanding tone. "I will enter Hell."

I squared off with Rocky for a few more heartbeats, then the great big dog flopped down onto his tummy and made a happy little whining noise.

"Thanks, buddy," I said, breathing a sigh of relief.

As I passed him, I gave each of his heads a scruffle and then headed further into Hell.

I paused at the tunnel leading from Cerberus' domain. It was there that Drake first kissed me. It was there I opened myself to feeling more for him. If I wanted to find him now, I was going to have to try to open myself up to him again. Him and the place he, even unwillingly, called home.

The magic – or whatever it was really called – of Hell had been a part of Drake, and his father. I'd been able to feel it, like a hum. Something almost out of reach to a mere human like me. But if I was accepting a life as Drake's wife, I was going to make it work for me. If I was a, for lack of a better word, princess of Hell now, Hell was going bend to my saved will.

I lay my hand over a patch of the wall, closed my eyes, took a deep breath, and concentrated.

After a few more breaths, I was sure it was working. I could see Drake pacing in his father's throne room. They were arguing about something–

"Ma'am?" Truman asked as Ignacio grunted, "What are you doing?"

"Shh," I whispered. "I'm trying to find Drake."

"And you think this will help…how?" Truman asked.

"I'm going to tap into the magic of Hell and…know things," I answered, still whispering.

"Ma'am–"

"Don't ruin it," Kyle said wistfully.

"I wouldn't," Truman said. "If there was anything to ruin. Are you sure that will work, ma'am?"

"Yes. I can see him."

"Of course, you can, ma'am."

I turned to Truman. "Are you suggesting my brain's making it up?"

"I wouldn't dare, ma'am. Why don't you lead the way then?"

I nodded. "Fine. I will." I pointed down another tunnel. "We go that way."

"After you, ma'am."

I headed off, full of confidence. I knew where Drake was and I was fairly certain I knew how to navigate the illogical pathways of Hell to get to him.

The brown stone of the tunnel faded as we walked out into an open field. It was grey. The people wandering around it seemingly aimlessly were grey. The grass and the sparse trees were grey.

"Well, that's a whole lot of…grey. Where are we?"

"The Asphodel Fields," Ignacio answered, sounding almost awed.

I looked down at him and saw him standing slightly behind me. "What's the matter?"

"The fields are full of the shades of the dead, ma'am," Truman said reverently. "Those who've drunk of the Lethe and forgotten their worldly lives."

A whispering on the wind teased my ears and I looked around for the source, my brain going pleasantly foggy. I felt my feet moving of their own accord as I trailed through the fields. Through the haze of fogginess in my head, I heard the boys calling me, I felt their claws trying gently to get my attention. But something stronger was calling me.

I felt something cold on my legs before I realised what was happening.

I blinked and looked down, seeing water coming up to my mid-calf.

"Serenity, get out!" Truman yelled at me.

I turned to look at him, but my foot caught on something in the murky water.

"Noooo!" I heard Kyle shout in slow-motion as I started falling.

But, before my head went under the water, a pair of strong arms grabbed me and hauled me up. I took a deep breath and realised I was on a long, narrow boat. I looked up and saw a tall figure in a hood.

"Charon, our lord will not be pleased you left your post."

"Neither will he be pleased to find his son's wife a shade." His voice was little more than the whispering of leaves, rustling along a footpath in an Autumn breeze.

"Okay," I said and they all turned to look at me. "I'm starting to feel like maybe I haven't mastered the magic of Hell."

"Whatever would have given you that idea, ma'am?"

I frowned at Truman and his thinly veiled sass. "Do you know the way to Drake?"

Truman bowed his head. "Charon can take us to the inner sanctum."

"I ferry the dead, hellspawn," Charon hissed. "And the stream of dead does not ebb."

"I'm sure our lord will be eternally grateful for the detour," Ignacio snapped with a snarl.

Charon's hood bobbed as though he was looking the devilbums over. "Then we will leave now. Keep her away from the sides until we are clear of the Lethe."

"I know how the rivers work, ferryman," Ignacio spat as he jumped from the bank to the boat.

Kyle squealed in delight as he hopped over, needing a claw from Ignacio to stop him falling into the water.

Truman traversed the gap as though it was nothing, with far more decorum than his little legs should have been capable of.

"You will want to sit, human," Charon said to me as he took up his pole again at his post at the back of the boat.

I stumbled to sitting as he started to punt the boat through the water with more strength and speed than any human would ever be able to manage.

Truman and Ignacio took up position on either side of me and Kyle climbed into my lap as we sailed smoothly down the river. The tempting whisperings brushed up against my mind, but the boys distracted me until we'd joined a much larger waterway.

"How long will it take to get there this way?" I asked Charon.

"It will take as long as it takes."

And it did. Which was not as long as the statement had made it sound. I was still dripping wet by the time we made landfall again, plus my clothes were ripped after a little sojourn through some rocks and some souls who got to spend all of eternity being drowned in the Styx.

So, I was tired and stressed and annoyed by the time I shoved open the double doors to Lucifer's throne room. I lifted my head, both hands still braced on the doors, and saw Drake and Lucifer paused in conversation.

"Serenity?" Lucifer asked.

21
Drake

My father was getting on my last nerve. I was about ready to stage a coup and take over the whole place myself. Anything to avoid one more Grandad-saved musical number in the name of cheering me up.

"Now, I think we should stage it as a mourning concert," Dad was saying.

I ran my hand over my face with a sigh. "Just get over it. She's gone and she's staying gone."

"I just don't see—"

We both turned at the sudden opening of the door and the person glaring at us was the last person I expected to see in the bowels of Hell.

"Serenity?" Dad asked as though he couldn't fathom that it was actually her.

And I was barely convinced myself. I couldn't be sure it wasn't just a figment created out of wishful thinking.

She was a mess. Her face was streaked and dirty. Her hair hung wet and limp. Her clothes were ripped and dripping. And, even through the exhaustion, she looked determined.

"Drake. We have to talk," she said, pulling her weight off the doors as though it was an effort.

"I…" I looked at my dad.

"No. No. By all means." Dad waved his hand towards Wren and nodded his head, then crossed his arms, his hand under his chin. "This whole thing is basically irrelevant now."

I threw him a glare and he shrugged.

"What? I just assumed."

"Why are you wet?" I asked her, so far from even trying to be sexy I surprised even myself.

"I…took a little dip in…a couple of rivers on the way here." She blew a piece of stray hair out of her eyes.

"You what?" I looked around for Truman and the boys, feeling anger bubbling.

"She's quite clearly fine, son. Why don't you two take this to your room?"

"Fine? How is she fine? She was…" I turned to her. "How are you fine?"

Wren sighed and crossed her arms. "I dunno. Maybe I channelled the magic of Hell after all." She stepped into the room fearlessly. "Can we do this, or what?"

I nodded. "Sure. Yeah."

Before I could take a step, Dad put his hand on my shoulder and leant his lips to my ear. "I'll organise a dinner, shall I?"

"Can you just…?" I sighed. I did not have the energy for two arguments. "Whatever makes you happy, old man."

I strode towards Wren, resisting the urge to pull her to me and kiss her hard. For starters, I didn't need my father breaking out the confetti and fireworks if I did. And secondly, I wasn't sure what talk she wanted to have. She'd braved the depths of Hell to get here, so I had to hope it was all good. But I'd learnt young not to make assumptions.

As I looked back out the door, I saw Truman and the boys hovering in the tunnel.

"You call this looking after her?" I asked, sparing them each an enquiring look.

"Master Drake–" Truman started but I shook my head.

"I will deal with you three later," I told them.

Kyle squeaked in panic and scurried to hide behind Ignacio, who's face barely shifted out of its usual scowl.

"Do not take it out on them!" Wren snapped as she slid her eyes to my father.

He wasn't even pretending not to listen.

"You've got an excuse," I told her. "They should know better."

"Excuse me?"

I paused before replying, wanting to steer this away from an argument if possible. "You've got an excuse for your hairbrained plan to get back into Hell. The three of them should have known better."

"My hairbrained plan got me here, didn't it?"

My eyes narrowed. "Exactly how did you get here relatively unscathed?"

She drew herself up defensively. "Now you care?"

"What is that supposed to mean?" I snapped, caring very little for the demons passing the room who were, like my father, doing a piss-poor job of not listening to our conversation.

"Might I remind you that you're the one who sent me back to Earth. I didn't ask to go–"

"You didn't ask to stay!" I growled, all devil.

She blanched, but stood her ground. Her jaw tightened as she glared at me furiously. There was no fear on her beautiful, dirt-streaked face. If she loved me, she would have made a truly perfect wife.

"You made it abundantly clear you didn't want me to stay, Drake. And forgive me for being too weak and *human* too stick it out under the assumption I wasn't wanted!"

"Wait. What?" I asked, frowning in confusion.

"Yes. I know. Stupid weak humans. We're so insecure in our mortal fragility to just take what we want." She stamped her foot and it surprised the Heaven out of me. "But damn it, I am Lucifer's daughter-in-law and I *will* take what I bloody well want. And you're just going to have to deal with it!"

For the first time in as long as I could remember, I was speechless. I was full of hope about what she was really saying, but I couldn't seem to form the words to check. I was powerless in the face of her, this human goddess.

She rolled her eyes and stormed towards me. "For Lucifer's sake, I'm telling you I love you, you stubborn idiot!" she huffed, then reached up and grabbed my face, pulling me down to kiss her.

It took me a moment to respond. Me. The son of the literal devil took a moment to respond to a gorgeous woman kissing him. I know. Not my finest moment by any stretch – and that was taking into account the centuries of torturing.

But once I had responded, I wrapped my arms around her and lifted her off the ground. When the kiss ended and she pulled back to look at me, I let her get her feet under her and put her down.

As I'd predicted, Dad let go the fireworks and more fucking glitter. He'd also pulled out some pom poms, but I wasn't going to focus on that. There was a woman in front of me, my wife, and she was waiting for me to speak.

I still didn't really know what to say. The words didn't come easily to me. I felt a grating against my skin at the very thought of them. They weren't in a hellspawn's vocabulary. Strictly, it was unsure if we were even capable – most still thought it was just extreme lust.

"Seriously?" Wren asked, taking one more step back. "Nothing?"

My throat felt tight. "It's not that I don't…" My tongue felt fat in my mouth.

"I trekked through the wilderness to be freaked out by a gatekeeper! I faced off against Cerberus! I fell in the freaking river Lethe! I fought drowning souls! And that's all I get?"

"It's not like I don't…"

"You either tell me you do or you don't, Drake. Or so help me, you'll never see me again."

"I do, Wren. I do."

She looked me over, finally breaking into a soft smile as she uncrossed her arms. "I'll take it."

I opened my arms and she ran into them. I lifted her up, actually feeling like the second round of fireworks and glitter was probably called for.

There was going to be a Heaven-load of shit to sort out if Wren was staying. But we had all the time in the world, and there was only one thing I wanted just then. And I could finally call her mine with absolutely no caveat and no deadline.

Dad was making up some kind of cheer routine in the background. So, I put my wife back down and turned to him. His cheerleading outfit was completed by pigtails. Wren's hand found mine and I squeezed it tight.

"Now can I plan the dinner? Please?" Dad begged, his pom poms together under his chin almost like he was praying to Grandad.

Wren laughed. "He is just like Mum."

Dad put a hand on his hip and the other under his chin as he struck a pose. "Does she also have legs for days?"

"Uh, no. But she is very keen on a celebration."

"Really?" Dad asked, failing at even faking nonchalance. "I like celebrations. What sort of celebration?"

"Actually…she wanted me to promise we'd have a real wedding."

Dad gasped, his cheerleading outfit being replaced with a prim, black tuxedo. "I *love* a wedding."

"We're already married," I reminded him.

Dad shook his head. "No. Well, yes. But…a party, Drake! We *have* to have a proper wedding!"

"I think Mum would settle for just a family dinner," Wren said, turning to me. "On Earth is probably better?"

I nodded. "I can do that. I'll do a family dinner if that'll make her happy."

"It sounds like a wedding will make her happy," Dad said grumpily and I knew he shared Wren's mum's sentiment.

"I…wouldn't say no to a wedding…" Wren said quietly. "I mean, if you…?"

I'd have thought I'd panic on hearing those words from her mouth. But I didn't. It was the opposite. Mostly.

I shrugged. "If it would make our parents happy…?"

"It's not a terrible reason?"

A smile broke out on her face that was mirrored on mine. "I guess we start with family dinner?"

Wren nodded. "Okay. Good start."

"We'll all go!" Dad said and we both looked at him. "I've *always* wanted to plan a wedding."

"You're…going to Earth?" Wren asked.

"Why not? We'll all have a great time!"

Good Uncle Jesus, the devil was going to walk the Earth.

"Announcement. Residents of Hell. This is your captain speaking. I will be absent for a few hundred years." Dad's voice boomed over the entirety of Hell. "We're going to have a wedding!" the devil cried gleefully.

Even Esther looked slightly less dour than usual, and I hadn't even realised she was in the room.

A slow, thundering clang boomed through my whole body, vibrating up through the soles of my boots and in every molecule around me.

The bells of Hell had rung only once in the time I'd been there. They'd signalled my arrival. Ringing in a new prince and a new epoch.

But there they went again, crashing through the whole of my father's domain.

This time, they were signalling far more than a new epoch.

Hell had a new princess. A human no less. She was here entirely of her own free will.

And she was all mine.

…continue the story in Book 2.

Damned if I do

You can check out the playlist for this series on Spotify. Just click or scan the QR code.

Thank you so much for reading this story! Word of mouth is super valuable to authors. So, if you have a few moments to rate/review Wren and Drake's story – or, even just pass it on to a friend – I would be really appreciative.

Have you looked for my books in store, or at your local or school library and can't find them? Just let your friendly staff member or librarian know that they can order copies directly from LightningSource/Ingram.

If you want to keep up to date with my new releases, rambles and writing progress, sign up to my newsletter at https://landing.mailerlite.com/webforms/landing/y1n6q2.

Follow me:

Thanks

I have so much thanks for this one. Not in the least for the ideas for coming so swift and easily, I'm already itching to get started on Book 2!

As always, the Beata Team – thanks in particular to Julie, Anna and Maria for fitting in my crunched deadline to give it a read. Your feedback was invaluable as always.

Thanks to Charny for letting me bounce ideas off her constantly and for being the main reason I now have about ten spin-offs to write.

And special thanks to Andy for getting started on the Christmas cheer for me while I was busy working. Thanks for organising to feed me and for looking after the animals and house, even though you were doing busy work, too.

My Books

Scarlett's list is just starting out, but you can find where to buy all my books in print and eBook at my website; www.elizabethstevens.com.au/.

About the Author

Scarlett Knox is the Paranormal Darker/Bully Romance penname of bestselling author Elizabeth Stevens. Scarlett is the name to read if you want darker/bully romance in the Mature YA/NA crossover space with paranormal elements. Think high school, college, and academy. Add in superpowers, vampires and werewolves, angels and demons, and more. Scarlett brings my usual wit, banter, and repartee in good old enemies-to-lovers showdowns between alpha males and the sassy heroines strong enough to kick them to their knees.

Writer. Reader. Perpetual student. Nerd.

Born in New Zealand to a Brit and an Australian, I am a writer with a passion for all things storytelling. I love reading, writing, TV and movies, gaming, and spending time with family and friends. I am an avid fan of British comedy, superheroes, and SuperWhoLock. I have too many favourite books, but I fell in love with reading after Isobelle Carmody's *Obernewtyn*. I am obsessed with all things mythological – my current focus being old-style Irish faeries. I live in Adelaide (South Australia) with my long-suffering husband, delirious dog, mad cat, two chickens, and a lazy turtle.

Contact me:

Email: scarlettknox@elizabethstevens.com.au
Website: www.elizabethstevens.com.au/scarlet-knox
Twitter: www.twitter.com/writer_iz
Instagram: www.instagram.com/writeriz
Facebook: https://www.facebook.com/elizabethstevens88/